"You have a  hands?"

Leah looked up as he, so close, and her breath caught on its way to give her words a voice. "Uh, yeah. Thanks for your help."

He smiled then, the first time she'd seen him smile, and it was the kind of thing that turned a reasonably intelligent woman into a blithering idiot.

"You said that already," he said.

"What?"

"You thanked me twice."

Her brain scrambled for an appropriate response. "Once for each hand?"

He laughed at that, making her smile, too.

Leah broke eye contact, her thoughts fixated on the man who had helped her. The feel of his strong arm around her shoulders, not allowing her to fall. The way his smile totally changed his face. And those blue eyes that drew her with a power that would scare her if she thought about it.

For tonight, she chose not to think about it.

Dear Reader,

We all probably know someone, or might even be that someone, who has endured a trauma that threatened to change who we are or our way of looking at the world. It takes strength and courage to get beyond that and reclaim the person we really are and the life we want. It definitely helps to have supportive, loving people by our side on that journey.

Leah Murphy in *A Rancher to Love* learns that truth when Tyler Lowe comes into her life at exactly the right time. I hope you enjoy their combined journey to happily-ever-after.

Trish Milburn

A RANCHER
TO LOVE

Trish Milburn

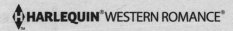
HARLEQUIN® WESTERN ROMANCE®

Recycling programs
for this product may
not exist in your area.

ISBN-13: 978-0-373-75626-1

A Rancher to Love

Copyright © 2016 by Trish Milburn

Printed in U.S.A.

Trish Milburn writes contemporary romance for the Harlequin Western Romance line and paranormal romance for the Harlequin Nocturne series. She's a two-time Golden Heart® Award winner, a fan of walks in the woods and road trips, and a big geek girl, including being a dedicated Whovian and Browncoat. And from her earliest memories, she's been a fan of Westerns, be they historical or contemporary. There's nothing quite like a cowboy hero.

Books by Trish Milburn

Harlequin American Romance

Elly: Cowgirl Bride
The Texan's Cowgirl Bride

Blue Falls, Texas

Her Perfect Cowboy
Having the Cowboy's Baby
Marrying the Cowboy
The Doctor's Cowboy
Her Cowboy Groom
The Heart of a Cowboy
Home on the Ranch

The Teagues of Texas

The Cowboy's Secret Son
Cowboy to the Rescue
The Cowboy Sheriff

Visit the Author Profile page
at Harlequin.com for more titles.

To Beth Pattillo and Page Pennington. Thanks for the help in brainstorming this and other Blue Falls stories at our MCRW winter retreat. Your ideas and support came right when I needed it.

Chapter One

Frustration and anxiety twisted Leah Murphy's middle as she sat outside the sheriff's department office. Which, of course, was completely irrational considering she was here to see her cousin Conner, one of the local deputies. But some part of her brain, the section that governed fight or flight, had her flashing back to the night when her apartment had been filled with uniformed officers.

No, she didn't want to think about that here. She'd come to Blue Falls to leave the memories behind, but they seemed determined to stay adhered to her every thought like a supremely unwelcome guest. Like one of those people who didn't understand the concept of personal space and insisted on invading it.

Leah gripped the steering wheel of her little crossover SUV and forced herself to take several deep… slow…breaths.

Her parents were concerned she was running from her problems and fears instead of confronting them, but she needed this. Needed the peace and calm and safety she'd always associated with Blue Falls. She looked out the windshield at the town's quintessential American Main Street in the distance and allowed herself to believe that violence never visited here. She knew that wasn't true. Every place, no matter the size and location, experienced violence of some type. But at least for now, she needed to believe the lie.

With another fortifying breath, she turned off the engine. Immediately, the Texas heat started to bake her like a potato in an oven with four wheels, prompting her to get out of the vehicle.

The door to the sheriff's department office opened, and Leah couldn't prevent a sharp intake of breath when a tall man stepped out. When would she stop being so jumpy? Then recognition hit the moment the man smiled at her, and she found herself smiling back at Sheriff Simon Teague.

"Hey, Leah. Conner said you were stopping by for a visit. I wanted to tell you that I got Keri one of your necklaces for her birthday and I earned major 'Good Husband' points. So thanks for that."

Leah chuckled a little, which felt foreign, like a language she'd once known but had largely forgotten because she hadn't used it in so long. She chose to look at it as a positive step, however small.

"Maybe that should be part of my business logo, 'Keeping Husbands Out of the Doghouse.'"

"Sales would skyrocket." Simon flashed another easy smile, making Leah think that Keri Teague was a lucky woman.

Leah wondered if she'd ever feel safe enough again to find her own happily-ever-after.

"Have a good visit." Simon tapped the brim of his tan hat and headed for his department SUV.

Beginning to feel as though her fair skin was blistering under the brutal late July sun, she walked inside. The blast of cold from the air-conditioning hit her as equal parts shocking and welcome. Even before her eyes adjusted to being out of the bright sunlight, she heard a voice she'd known her entire life.

"Hey, cuz," Conner said as he walked up to her and pulled her in to one of his bear hugs. After the initial, involuntary stiffening at being touched, she slowly relaxed and had to fight tears at how good it felt to see him, to be wrapped in the familiar embrace. Though they'd never lived in the same place, they'd always been close, having been born only a month apart. Though it had always been annoying how he crowed about being older than her. Brat.

"So what brings you out from the big city?" Conner released her and stepped back.

Leah glanced around the office and saw one other deputy she didn't recognize—probably the replacement for Pete Kayne, who was a state trooper now and on his way to eventually becoming a Texas Ranger.

"Can we talk in private?"

The way Conner's eyes widened a fraction told her the question surprised him, but then he nodded and motioned for her to follow him to the room they used for everything from lunch to interrogations.

Conner closed the door once they were in the room. She sank onto one of the chairs, the familiar exhaustion that came from lack of sleep weighing on her.

Conner sat in the chair at the end of the table next to her. "What's up?"

Leah swallowed. "I was wondering if I could stay with you for a little while."

Conner's brows moved toward each other. "Wouldn't you rather stay in Mom and Dad's guest room?"

"No, I… I don't really feel up to a lot of questions right now. And even though I asked Mom not to say anything, I wouldn't doubt she's talked to Aunt Charlotte."

"About what?"

Leah picked at the cuticle on her thumb. "My apartment was broken into a couple of weeks ago, and… I was attacked."

"Attacked?" Conner sat more rigid in his seat and asked the single-word question in a tone that said he was afraid of the answer.

She clasped her hands together. "Just some bumps and bruises, but… I can't sleep there. I had to leave."

"God, Leah, did they catch the guy?"

She nodded. "I managed to get my hand on his neck and pushed his head back against the coffee table. It gave me time to get away." Barely. She swallowed against the lump in her throat threatening to cut off her breath. "The police arrived then."

Brought by the call of a neighbor who'd heard crashing and her initial screams before her attacker had thrown her down on the couch and started tugging at her clothes. Chills scurried across her skin, and she rubbed against them to try to ward off the feeling of Jason Garton's breath much too close, the rough way he'd pulled at her shorts, the primal fear for her life. The horror of the idea that she might be raped. And killed.

She couldn't speak the details, not even to Conner. Not even to her mother. The only person she'd told was the female officer who'd escorted her into Leah's kitchen and gently asked for an account of what had happened.

"Are you okay?" The concern in Conner's voice was almost her undoing. Typically they were more likely to joke with each other, so to hear something so different, so sincere, caused that damn lump in her throat to balloon in size.

"I will be." She hoped. Some days she literally jumped at her own shadow, then felt like a fool for doing so.

"I'd let you stay at my apartment, but I'm actually staying with Mom and Dad for a few days. My apartment flooded, and they're having to replace the flooring and some of the drywall."

Leah's heart sank. She loved her aunt and uncle, but she wouldn't find the peace and quiet she needed at their house. They would mean well—just like her parents did—but the idea of them constantly checking on her, always just being there, was more than she could handle right now.

"We can see if Skyler has any openings at the Wildflower Inn. How long are you going to be here?"

Tension knotted in her stomach as she realized she was going to have to tell him her plans sooner than she expected. That this was more than a visit. Though her parents thought she was acting too hastily, something inside her knew her decision to leave Houston and take up residence in Blue Falls was the right one. Even with Jason Garton behind bars, she still suffered from panic attacks each time she stepped into her apartment. Her rational brain knew the likelihood of yet another intruder lying in wait was miniscule, but that message didn't get through to the place fear resided, ready to pounce at the least provocation.

Here she hoped she could feel safe and be far

enough away from the noise and bustle of Houston that she could finally start thinking like a rational human being again. That she could reclaim the happy, creative, fun-loving person she'd always been.

"I'm not going back to Houston." Just saying the words made it more real, and she didn't know whether to be relieved or scared that she was losing her mind. Maybe the right answer was both.

Conner stared at her for a moment, and she feared a barrage of questions or that he would caution her against acting too rashly. Instead, he simply nodded.

"What are you looking for?"

The relief that washed over her made tears threaten. "I want peace and quiet, some solitude without being too alone." She shook her head at her inability to properly vocalize the feeling of what she needed. "That probably doesn't make sense."

A jolt of her anxiety returned. In her mind, she really hadn't examined options beyond staying with Conner. With him she thought she might feel safe. She feared being alone again, even in a different town. What if she felt just as scared in Blue Falls as she did Houston? What if the fear never went away?

Not wanting to hop that train of thought, Leah pushed the fears aside. She knew they'd reassert themselves later, but for now she wanted to enjoy a reprieve.

"It does make sense," Conner said. "And I think I know the perfect place."

TYLER LOWE WATCHED his five-year-old niece sitting on the opposite side of his kitchen table nibbling on her grilled cheese sandwich, quiet as the proverbial church mouse.

"Maddie, is the sandwich okay?" He wasn't a fancy chef, but he thought he made a mean grilled cheese.

Maddie nodded but didn't speak. She'd been like this for the past month, ever since her mother had dropped her on his doorstep almost without taking time to stop the beat-up car she was driving. His fists tightened as the familiar anger at his younger sister rushed to the surface again. Kendra had always been flighty, a handful for their parents, but she'd graduated to unfit mother when she'd started drinking and taking drugs. It was a sad state of affairs when a single rancher and farrier with no experience raising children was preferable to a child's own mother.

Even so, each day he felt more like an abject failure. What had his niece endured that had turned her from a happy, energetic toddler to the quiet child who almost seemed scared of him? Once upon a time, she'd crawl up on his lap and pat his face with her chubby little fingers. But she likely didn't remember that. Now she was no longer energetic or chubby, and he was just a guy her mother had left her with, someone she didn't know anymore.

And he had no idea how to reach her.

He reverted back to silence, too, thinking how he needed to take her shopping for new clothes soon. Not surprising that Kendra had left the child behind with only one small bag of clothes and the stuffed puppy that was never far from Maddie's side. Since her arrival, he'd bought her a few things. But with school right around the corner, she needed not only clothes and shoes but also school supplies. And when had school supply lists become as long as his arm, and for a kindergartner? Evidently she had to have everything from crayons to safety scissors to boxes of tissues.

A little more than a month ago, he'd have never thought he'd be enrolling a child in kindergarten for the fall. He was about as equipped to be a parent as a bull was to fly jumbo jets. And he was discovering that raising a kid was expensive, even if you just provided the basics. No wonder his sister had left her only child in his care. Yes, it was an unkind thought, but abandoning Maddie had been the last straw.

"Honey, why don't you wrap up the other half of your sandwich and bring it with you?"

Maddie met his gaze, a tentative question in her pretty green eyes.

"I've got to go to another ranch to work on a horse's feet." And of course there was no way he was leaving a five-year-old home alone. He didn't think a babysitter was a good idea either, at least not yet. His gut told him that being left with yet another person she didn't know wasn't the best thing for Maddie right now. He might not know what was, but that wasn't it.

Maddie slipped out of her chair and wrapped her sandwich in a napkin. She held it in one hand and her puppy in the other. She didn't even question that she had to go with him, which some instinct told him wasn't normal. Weren't kids her age normally full of questions, curiosity on steroids?

God, he hoped he figured out how to communicate with her soon. It was like living with a child who'd very nearly taken a vow of silence.

Maddie kept her sandwich wrapped as he drove toward town, but she did seem to be interested in the countryside. She sat up straight in the booster seat he'd gotten her.

He pointed across a field. "The couple who live in that house raise little horses. They're only about as tall as you. Maybe we can go and see them sometime. Would you like that?"

Maddie hesitated for a minute but then nodded.

Okay, that was a tiny positive step. He wanted to ask her why she didn't speak any more than she did, but he hoped waiting and being kind to her would lead to her speaking on her own. Maybe starting school next month would help. She'd be around other kids her age, at her level. He just crossed his fingers that the experience didn't freak her out too much, the way it had Kendra when she'd started school. The school had called his mom because Kendra wouldn't stop crying. It had taken what seemed like forever to his eight-year-old mind for his sister to stop bawling like a baby at school.

As they continued into town and then down Main Street, Maddie seemed to soak up all the sights. The people on the sidewalks, the displays in the windows, everything. There was a curious little girl in there if he could just figure out a way to get her to come out.

He spotted the small ice-cream stand that sat near the lake. Every kid liked ice cream, right?

"Hey, would you like an ice-cream cone?"

Maddie looked at him and he could tell from the bright look in her eyes that she wanted to say yes.

"I think I'll have one, too. I like peach flavor. What do you like?"

"Strawberry." Her response was almost a whisper, but at least it was something.

"Strawberry, good choice."

They waited in line behind a small group of women who, judging by the bags they held, were in town for a day of shopping. When it was his and Maddie's turn, he placed the order.

"This must be your niece."

He turned at the sound and saw Verona Charles with her own niece, Elissa Kayne. "Yes, this is Maddie."

Verona smiled as she leaned down to eye level with Maddie. "Well, aren't you just the prettiest little thing."

Maddie remained quiet, and he sensed that part of her wanted to take a step away from the other woman. Too many new people coming into her life too quickly.

"It's nice to meet you, Maddie," Elissa said, speaking to her in a normal adult tone, not that cutesy kid voice most people used.

"You, too." Two whole words. Progress.

Tyler met Elissa's gaze, and he saw the questions there. But she was kind enough not to pry. No doubt the whole county had heard how Kendra had abandoned her daughter. He really hoped that knowledge didn't trickle down to any of the kids who would be Maddie's classmates because kids could be cruel to each other. And even though he didn't know the specifics, he knew in his gut that Maddie had been through enough.

When their ice cream was handed through the window, he grabbed them and extended Maddie's to her. She immediately took an enthusiastic lick, making him smile.

"She's got the right idea," Verona said. "Give me a double scoop of strawberry."

As Verona started to turn toward him, he said, "We better be off. Work calls."

The thing about living in a small town and everyone knowing your business was that you knew theirs, as well. And the mission in life for Verona Charles was to make sure she paired up every single person within a twenty-mile radius of Blue Falls. No, thank you. If he ever got married, it would be to a woman of his choosing with no outside prompting. But right now marriage was the furthest thing from his mind, although the thought had flitted through his noggin more than once that maybe having a wife would make Maddie's transition easier.

But he wasn't even dating anyone, so he'd have to figure this out on his own.

As he drove toward the ranch where he'd be working this afternoon, he let his thoughts wander over ways to up his income. He got along fine by himself plying his trade as a farrier and running a small herd of cattle. But things had changed the moment Maddie had become his responsibility. He supposed he could advertise his farrier services farther out from Blue Falls, but he figured most people with horses in the area already knew about him.

Maybe he'd get lucky and someone would rent the bunkhouse. The rental notice he'd put up on the community bulletin board at the Primrose Café had been up less than twenty-four hours, but he kept hoping it would bear fruit.

The bunkhouse had sat unused other than for some storage for years, so it made sense to try to make it generate some income. It wasn't fancy, but it was sturdy and had a good roof.

Sure, he'd have to deal with someone else coming and going from the ranch, but it seemed the most expedient way of getting what he needed for his niece now and for however long she was with him. Kendra hadn't said when she'd be back for her daughter, and Tyler wasn't sure his sister would even remember she had a child. He knew one thing for sure. No way was Maddie going with her mother unless he was convinced Kendra had gotten her act together and was clean.

He glanced over at Maddie as she licked her ice cream. He might feel like a clueless wonder regarding how to interact with her, but there was no denying he'd do whatever he had to in order to protect her and give her what she needed, two things he feared his sister hadn't done in a long time.

Just as he parked next to the barn where he'd be working the next couple of hours, his phone rang. When he answered, Conner Murphy was on the other end of the call.

"I saw where your bunkhouse is for rent," Conner said. "Is it still available?"

"It is. You looking to move out of town?"

"No, it's for my cousin Leah."

Now that he had an actual bite on the bunkhouse, Tyler experienced a moment of doubt about having someone else on his land. But he glanced over at Maddie and thought about how much easier it would be to provide for her with extra income. He had the feeling she had wanted for a lot in her young life, and he didn't want that to continue while she was under his roof.

After he and Conner discussed a few particulars, they set a time for Leah Murphy to come see the bunkhouse.

Tyler knew nothing about Conner's cousin, but because of Maddie he felt better about possibly having a woman living next door than a man. He just hoped he was making the right decision about having anyone there at all. Though Maddie would likely have little or no interaction with his tenant, it was still another change. And the way he saw things, he and Maddie had both had enough changes for a good long while.

Chapter Two

Leah's stomach churned at what suddenly felt like a ride on a runaway roller coaster. She hadn't expected to find a potential new home so soon. If she were honest, she'd hoped it would take a while, time during which she could prepare herself for living alone again. Having to face that less than an hour after arriving in Blue Falls hadn't remotely been part of her plan.

Leah knew she should be thankful, should take this as a sign that her decision to move to Blue Falls was the right one. Besides, there was no guarantee waiting longer would make the transition any easier. And the truth was that even if Conner's place wasn't currently uninhabitable, it was too small for two people who weren't a couple and didn't mind the close quarters.

"Tyler said he wouldn't be home for a couple of hours, so what do you say we go grab something to eat?"

Leah didn't feel much like eating, but what else was she going to do to pass the time? Attempting to eat and talking with her cousin sure sounded better than sitting around waiting and allowing her anxiety to grow.

"You can't beat that for timing," Conner said as

they headed down the street to the Primrose Café. "And Tyler's a good guy."

But a guy nonetheless.

Not wanting to appear ungrateful for Conner's understanding and willingness to jump right in to help her, she gave him a smile. "Thank you."

"That's what awesome cousins are for."

Her smile grew into a genuine one. She appreciated his levity.

Somehow she made it through the meal, managing to say the appropriate things at the appropriate times, both to Conner and all the friendly locals. By the time Conner had to head back to work, she was thankful for the blessed quiet of her car. When she slipped into the driver's seat, she simply sat for several minutes, watching the comings and goings of the people who were going to be her new neighbors.

Using her phone, she pulled up a map of Tyler Lowe's address. Conner had told her the bunkhouse wasn't far from Lowe's house. He'd shared that fact in a tone that meant he thought that would assure her, but once again her stomach twisted into knots.

Lowe's ranch was a few miles out of town. Sure, she'd wanted peace and quiet, but would being out that far alone be even more frightening than what she'd left behind? If someone attacked her there, would there be anyone close by to hear her scream?

She shook her head, telling herself for the umpteenth time that just because she'd been attacked once didn't mean it would ever happen again. Realistically, it probably meant the chances were less than they'd been initially. Plus, if there were fewer people around, didn't that mean there was less of a chance that one of them would be the type to attack her in the first place?

The what-if game could drive her mad if she let it, so she gave herself a mental smack and looked in the rearview mirror. She smoothed her hair and made sure she didn't look like death. She needed to convey "I'm a responsible adult who pays her rent on time."

At least she hoped she could pay her rent on time. Thus, the need for getting her mind off what had happened and back on work. On finding her creative spirit again.

She paused with her hand clasping the keys in her ignition and took a slow, deep, calming breath before she ventured toward a new part of her life. On her way to her destination, she ran positive thoughts through her head. She would love this new place. She could afford it. She would feel safe and refreshed, inspired to create even more beautiful jewelry to sell in retail shops and online. It would feel like home.

When she reached the mailbox with the appropriate address, she turned off the highway onto a gravel drive that curved a couple of times before revealing a modest-sized house that had a few decades on it. Beyond it sat a barn and another structure that looked like a small wooden house with a low porch running the length of the front. That must be the bunkhouse, she guessed.

She talked down the part of her that wanted to turn around and retreat back to the safety of Conner's presence. Common sense prevailed as she spotted a dark blue pickup truck parked in the shade, telling her that Tyler Lowe was most likely inside one of the buildings. When anxiety tried tying her insides in knots again, she reminded herself that Conner had told her Lowe was a good man. She had to trust that her cousin would never put her in harm's way, especially not after she'd told him what had driven her to Blue Falls in the first place.

Of course, she hadn't told him everything. She didn't plan to ever share that with anyone she didn't have to in order to make sure her attacker stayed in jail for as long as possible. Reliving those horrible minutes made her skin crawl.

Rallying the friendly personality that had been second nature to her before the attack, she slipped out of her car and went in search of Tyler Lowe. Her first instinct would be to approach the house, but a metallic banging drew her to the barn instead. As she crossed the space between where she'd parked and the barn entrance, the sound stopped. Her nerves started firing again, more so with each step she took toward the barn. What if Conner was wrong about Lowe?

Stop it!

Common sense told her that not all men were the type who'd attack a woman. After all, she'd gone more than twenty-nine years without being assaulted by any man whose path she crossed. She'd simply become the unlucky victim in the statistics game.

Leah approached the open barn door, determined to greet Tyler Lowe with her friendliest smile. She hadn't counted on nearly colliding with a giant.

Her feet slipped on the gravel at the same time she gasped at the size of the man who'd stepped out of the barn. He reached toward her, probably to keep her from falling, but the gesture sent warning bells to clanging in her head and she managed to evade his touch. She took a couple of steps back as she righted herself.

"Sorry," he said in a deep voice that matched his impressive height and solid build. "Didn't mean to startle you."

After a couple of moments in which Leah fought hard against the visceral need to spin around and race toward her car, she somehow managed to wave off his concern. "It's okay. I... I'm looking for Tyler Lowe."

"You found him. Leah Murphy?"

She nodded, trying not to think about how the man in front of her was easily twice her size, maybe more, and could crush her without breaking a sweat.

He extended his hand and smiled. "Conner said you'd be coming by. Nice to meet you."

Even though his smile seemed genuine, not the evil type her attacker had worn, it was all she could do to force her own hand toward his for a shake. The moment his big, undeniably strong hand wrapped around her much smaller one, panic exploded inside her. What if he didn't let her go?

But after a quick shake, he thankfully released her. Judging by the curious look he gave her, she wouldn't be surprised if he thought her a complete lunatic. She needed to pull herself together if she wanted to even have the choice of whether to rent this place.

"You, too," she finally said.

"Come on," he said with a nod to his right. "I'll show you the place. It's nothing fancy, but it's in good physical shape. Has lots of space."

When Lowe started walking along the gravel drive that led past the barn, her brain didn't seem to want to send the appropriate message to her feet to follow him. Before he noticed her hesitation, she hurried to catch up. Of course, that was easier said than done considering his long legs easily outpaced hers without him even seeming to try.

As she tried to close the distance between them, she noticed just how wide his shoulders were, how solidly built he seemed to be. His tanned arms were no doubt strong if the cut of the muscles were any indication. His worn jeans clung to obviously muscled thighs and, she had to admit, a nicely made backside. Even with her nerves doing their best to overwhelm her, she still wasn't blind to the fact that Tyler Lowe was a finely made man not much older than her, if she was guessing correctly. There was no hint of the older man she'd for some reason assumed him to be when Conner had told her he had a place for rent.

"This used to be the bunkhouse for the ranch hands when my father and grandfather had more acreage and ran a bigger herd," he said as he stepped onto the long porch.

She imagined the inside as sparsely furnished and smelling like a locker room.

When Lowe opened the front door and motioned for her to precede him inside, her panic ratcheted up a notch. How could she possibly allow herself to be trapped inside by a man she didn't know? But then she remembered the pepper spray in her purse and held on to the strap even tighter as she forced her foot across the threshold.

The main room into which she stepped wasn't going to be featured on the cover of any home decorating magazines, but it wasn't as bad as she'd imagined it either. The room was filled with an older couch and chairs toward the front and a kitchen area on the back side. A long, wood, farm-style table and accompanying wood, ladder-back chairs divided the two areas. Off to the sides were doors leading to what appeared to be a couple of bedrooms and a bathroom.

"If you take it, feel free to spruce it up however you like. Doesn't exactly have a feminine feel to it."

No, it didn't. But already she was imagining spreading out her work along that long table and having more space to store her supplies. That was a good sign considering she'd been completely unable to work since the attack.

Leah crossed the room and looked into the bedrooms and bath. Definitely an older feel, like it hadn't been used in a while and needed a good airing out, but the space was nice and it was quiet. Still, she wondered if her mind and her fear would let her relax here, feel safe as she once had in her apartment.

She told herself she wouldn't know the answer to those types of questions unless she took the leap. She had to live somewhere, and it wasn't going to be Houston or her cousin's couch. She turned to face the man who seemed to take up an inordinate amount of space in the room.

"You live there?" she asked as she gestured in the direction of the house down the drive.

He nodded. "I do. But you'll have plenty of privacy. I do work on the ranch, but I'm gone a fair amount, too. I'm a farrier, so I'm called out to other ranches."

Even so, would she be able to find any calm with him so close by? She considered telling him she'd think about it and then look for something in town, but a part of her just wanted to have the decision done.

"I'll take it."

Her answer seemed to surprise him for a moment before he nodded. "Good."

They talked a bit about the rental agreement, and the fact that it was simply verbal without all the paperwork a place in the city required eased her concern some. The simplicity of life in a place like Blue Falls was just what she needed. She'd just have to get used to seeing Tyler Lowe and not imagining how easily he could hurt her.

TYLER HAD TO focus way harder than he should as Leah asked him how soon she could move in. But he really couldn't be blamed for how difficult he was finding it to talk about mundane rental details when facing a woman as beautiful as Leah Murphy, could he?

Somehow he found the correct responses as his gaze roamed over her wavy, honey-blond hair and the pink tinge to her fair skin. He towered over her, and he wondered if it made her nervous. The way she eyed him and kept her distance made him think so. Which he supposed was understandable. He doubted he'd be comfortable around someone double his size and at least a foot taller than him either.

As they exited the bunkhouse, he wondered if he'd made a mistake renting it to the first person to express an interest. The last thing he needed right now was a distraction, and Leah Murphy was definitely that. He'd known Conner for years, so how in the world had he never met his stunning cousin?

Maybe he wouldn't see her that often. Like he'd said, he was gone a good amount. And now he had Maddie to care for. Plus, Leah would have her own work. What did she do anyway? It had to be something that would allow her to move to a town as small as Blue Falls.

He glanced back at the bunkhouse as they walked away from it. He should be thankful he'd rented the place so quickly. The extra income would alleviate his concerns about providing for Maddie, and the bunkhouse had just been sitting there empty for a long time.

And he wasn't exactly sure why he thought so, but something told him that Leah needed the place as much as he needed to rent it. Her reasons weren't any of his business, but he couldn't deny the curiosity. Conner had mentioned she'd lived in Houston. Moving to Blue Falls was a big change, and people usually had big reasons for that type of move.

As they reached her car, he noticed how she opened the door and placed it between them before she turned to speak to him.

"Thank you," she said simply.

"It's me should be thanking you."

A hint of a smile tugged at the edge of her lips, enough that it had him wanting to know what she'd look like with a full smile.

Yeah, he was going to have to stay really busy.

Chapter Three

Leah jerked awake gasping for air, panic flooding her body. She scanned her surroundings, certain that Jason Garton was hiding in the unfamiliar shadows, on the verge of leaping out and finishing what he'd started. She lifted her hand to her neck, where she could still feel the tight grip of Garton's large fingers pressing her down, preventing her from escaping.

Gradually, her heart rate slowed as she remembered where she was—her new home on Tyler Lowe's ranch. After a couple of days at her parents' house while she made arrangements for her move, she'd dared to hope the nightmares about her attack were past. All it took for them to return with a vengeance was a single night alone in the bunkhouse.

Knowing from experience that she wouldn't be able to fall asleep again, she threw off the thin quilt and got out of bed. With her pulse still faster than normal, she made the round of doors and windows, making sure they were all locked. Then knowing she was being paranoid, she checked all the rooms, including the closets. No Jason Garton. No threats of any kind, unless she counted the threat of possibly stubbing her toe on one of the boxes containing her belongings.

Holding her breath, she eased to the window closest to the front door and peeked out through the blinds. The night was pitch-black except for the lone security light that hung on a post between the house and the barn. Even Tyler's house was dark. No doubt he was sound asleep as she should be. But then he probably didn't have nightmares about being attacked in his own home, his very life at risk.

She released the blind, allowing it to fall back into place, and turned back toward the pile of boxes Conner had helped her unload earlier in the day. If she couldn't sleep, she might as well make some progress on her unpacking before she convinced herself moving here had been a colossal mistake, solving nothing.

Tackling one box after another, she began to turn the bunkhouse into something resembling an actual home. Her clothes hanging in the closet, her dishes filling the kitchen cabinets, the patchwork quilt her grandmother had made for her draped over the back of the couch. When she reached the first of the boxes that held her jewelry-making supplies, she ran her hand across the plastic containers of colorful beads. The Swarovski crystals, pewter beads and Czech glass normally had her creativity tripping over itself with ideas. But that was before the night her life had been turned inside out, before the attack that had resulted in hundreds of her beads being catapulted in all directions as she'd tried desperately to reach something to free herself from Garton's grip.

"No!"

She growled in frustration and pressed the heels of her hands against her temples, wishing she could banish memories of that night. Defying that core of fear that refused to leave her alone, she pulled out her supplies and filled the long dining table with boxes of beads, wire and assorted tools of her trade. She might not be ready to get back to work tonight, but she would not hide her supplies away anymore. They'd given her countless hours of enjoyment and the ability to make a living, much more than the one night they were tainted. She needed to remember that, remind herself as many times as necessary.

When she finally got everything unpacked, she noticed the windows didn't look quite so dark anymore. A quick check through the blinds revealed the first pale light of day making its way across the ranch.

Leah considered collapsing back into bed. Maybe she'd become one of those people who slept during the day and kept night-owl hours for her work. But she'd always been someone who liked the early hours of the day when the world seemed to come alive again. Deciding to stay up and just call it an early night, she set a pot of coffee to brewing and took a quick shower. Maybe today was the day she'd really and truly reclaim her life and dive back into work.

Freshly showered and wearing clean clothes, she poured herself a cup of coffee and went out to sit in one of the old rocking chairs on her porch. She listened to the simple sounds of early morning, the birds chirping and a slight breeze stirring the tops of the trees on the opposite side of the gravel drive. She took a sip of her coffee and glanced to her right, noticing that the gravel ended a few yards beyond the bunkhouse but the drive continued on as a dirt surface until it reached a gate at the corner of the pasture. In the distance, she noticed a few head of cattle meandering out of the morning's disappearing shadows.

Even though she hadn't been able to sleep the night before, this slice of peacefulness was more than welcome. Maybe she just needed more time to adjust, to find her way back to some normalcy.

The sound of footsteps had her jerking her attention in the opposite direction. The source of the sound proved to be Tyler striding from the house toward the barn. He didn't look in her direction, giving her the opportunity to observe him from a distance. Now that he wasn't so close, he didn't seem so huge or imposing. Truthfully, her impression of his size had more to do with her own. It didn't take much to tower over someone who was only a couple of inches over five feet. If she could keep him this far away, maybe she'd be able to relax more and not suffer from the irrational fear that he posed a threat.

From the safety of her porch, she thought about how differently she would have viewed Tyler had they met before the attack. Well, pretty much the same in the looks department. Despite her nervousness around him, she wasn't blind to how handsome he was with those long, powerful legs, broad shoulders, nicely muscled arms. His short blond hair was a couple of shades darker than her own. But it was those blue eyes of his that could stop a woman in her tracks. She'd always been a sucker for a beautiful pair of eyes on a man, and Tyler Lowe definitely had that.

Too bad she wasn't sure she'd ever be comfortable around a man again. Not for the first time she wished she were taller, stronger, more able to protect herself.

Should she make an attempt to get to know Tyler?

Befriend him? Would it help her past her fear or just compound it? She sighed as the parade of questions about her future picked up speed in her mind.

After leisurely enjoying her coffee, she faced the fact that she couldn't simply sit on the porch all day. She had to be productive, take another step into her new life. When she realized she was waiting to catch another glimpse of Tyler, she forced herself inside the bunkhouse. Ready or not, she had to work. Though he seemed like a nice enough guy based on their limited interactions, she doubted Tyler would let her stay in her current accommodations for free.

She eyed the supplies on the table, hoping inspiration would strike. When her creative side stayed on hiatus, she instead started making a list of other tasks she could tackle in the meantime. Most important, she needed to arrange for internet access and go buy some groceries. What she'd brought from her apartment wouldn't last more than a day or maybe two if she stretched it.

Wanting to keep her distance, she texted Tyler to ask if he had any issue with her getting internet access set up at the bunkhouse. She found herself staring at her phone, waiting for the answer. When none came, she set it aside and began writing out her grocery list. That was a normal activity, and hopefully it would be another step toward leaving the attack and the fear in the past.

The sound of what she assumed was Tyler's voice drew her to the window. Maybe he was on the phone and that's why he hadn't texted her back yet.

But when she looked toward the house, she saw him walking toward his truck, a little blonde girl at his side. The child couldn't be more than five or six years old.

Leah didn't remember him saying anything about having a child, and now she wondered if Tyler was married. Was there a wife in the house whom she also hadn't seen? That certainly made her feel bad about appreciating how good-looking Tyler was, but having another woman on the ranch might help Leah relax and grow more comfortable around her landlord.

Despite the fact he might very well be a married man, Leah couldn't pull her gaze away from Tyler as he helped the little girl into the truck and fastened her in to her seat. Was there anything sexier than a handsome man caring for a small child?

Tyler shut the door and glanced toward the bunkhouse. Leah squeaked and stepped back from the window. Thank goodness she wasn't still sitting on the porch staring at him. She didn't need him or a potential wife seeing that, not if she didn't want to be packing up to move out a day after moving in.

She waited until she heard Tyler's truck start up and leave before she grabbed her grocery list, purse and keys and headed to her own vehicle. As she drove past the house, she glanced at the windows but saw no one. It struck her as strange that she didn't know whether to be disappointed or grateful.

As she drove into Blue Falls a few minutes later, the tightness of her muscles relaxed. The combination of daylight, a good number of people going about their business, and the warmth she'd always felt this community generated allowed her to breathe more easily. It also made her wonder if she'd made a mistake moving out into the country alone.

Leah shook her head as she drove through the downtown area. She was "borrowing trouble," as her mother was fond of saying. Neither Tyler nor her new home had truly given her any reason for concern. She was just allowing the dark parts of her imagination to run wild. Rather than working or settling into her new community, the top item on her to-do list was to stop imagining the worst was going to happen. She was allowing Jason Garton to continue to victimize her even though he was sitting in a jail cell more than two hundred miles away. And that made her angry more than anything else.

She parked at the grocery store and headed inside, determined to make today, her first as a full-time Blue Falls resident, a good one. In fact, she was in the mood to bake something sinfully delicious and headed straight for the baking aisle. She decided on caramel brownies and tossed the necessary ingredients in her cart then headed toward the next aisle.

"Leah!"

She jumped but then realized she recognized the female voice. India Parrish stood in between the end of the aisle Leah had just left and the meat counter along the back wall.

"Hey, India. How are you?"

"Great." India glanced at Leah's cart. "So it's true? You've moved to Blue Falls?"

Leah nodded. "Yeah, brand-new resident as of yesterday."

"That's awesome, and just in time. I'm down to the last piece of your jewelry in my shop."

"Glad to hear it's selling." Her bank account would

be equally as happy. And speaking of, she supposed she needed to transfer that, as well.

"Like hotcakes. I tried placing another order a few days ago, but I hadn't heard anything in response."

"Oh, sorry about that. Been having some site issues." As in she'd barely looked at it since the attack. "I'm actually in the process of getting reconnected here, so I'll get your order to you as soon as I can."

Which meant she had to work no matter if she felt inspired or not.

India waved her hand in a dismissive gesture. "No worries. I'm sure you have lots to do to get settled. I heard you rented the old bunkhouse out at Tyler Lowe's place."

"Yeah." Leah resisted the urge to ask India about Tyler, to get a second opinion on whether he was a good guy, safe to be around, whether he was married.

India waved at a blonde Leah didn't know, and the other woman carried her hand basket over to where they stood.

"Gina, this is Leah Murphy. She's the one who makes the beautiful jewelry I've had in the front display case at the shop. Leah, Gina Tolbert."

Gina extended her hand for a shake. "You do lovely work. I had my eye on a lapis and pearl necklace of yours, but I waited too long and someone snapped it up. That'll teach me to hesitate when I see something I want."

"I'm sure you could convince Leah to make another for you," India said with a smile that accentuated her natural beauty.

"Of course." Maybe if she forced herself to start

working again, it would actually take her mind off the things she didn't want to think about in the first place.

"Leah has just moved here." India met Leah's eyes. "Gina has only been here a few months herself."

"I've spent some time here over the years, though. My mom moved here when I was in my senior year of high school, when she got remarried. Though I stayed in Waco with my dad so I could finish school with my friends."

"We're lucky to have Gina here now, though," India said. "She's the new head of the tourist bureau, and she's got so many great ideas to keep the local economy booming that she's got all of our heads spinning."

As the two women told Leah about the addition of photography classes by the local-wildflower tour company, the budding wedding industry, and how the rodeo crowds were growing and thus drawing bigger-name talent, Leah couldn't help feeling their excitement.

India placed her hand atop Leah's where it sat gripping the handle of the shopping cart. "And this will be perfect for you. We're planning to have an arts and crafts trail soon where tourists can follow a map from one artist or craftsperson's shop to the next. They can watch the artists at work and buy their wares. I can see you being really successful with that, as long as I still get some of your stuff for Yesterwear."

"I can get you what information we have so far," Gina said.

"Thank you." In theory, Leah liked the idea a lot. But just thinking about strangers showing up at her doorstep had her stomach clenching and her skin prickling with chills. Not to mention the fact that it wasn't truly her home to do with as she liked. She doubted Tyler wanted strangers coming and going all the time, especially when he had a child's safety to consider.

"So what brought you to Blue Falls?" Gina asked.

Leah forced a small smile. "Just ready for a change. And I've always liked it here."

"Leah is Conner Murphy's cousin."

If she hadn't been looking at Gina, Leah would have missed the slight widening of her eyes. In a blink, the reaction was gone. What was that about? Hmm, perhaps she needed to ask her cousin about the pretty Miss Tolbert.

"Sorry to run, but I've got a meeting in twenty minutes." Gina gave a little wave and headed off toward the front of the store.

"I should finish up, too," Leah said. "Based on this conversation, I've evidently got lots of work to do."

India gave her a quick hug. "Don't forget what I said about the arts and crafts trail. It could really introduce your work to a lot of new people if it's as successful as we hope it'll be."

"I'll think about it." She couldn't promise more than that.

"When you get settled, give me a call or drop by the shop. We'll have lunch."

"Sounds good." And it did, but Leah suddenly felt exhausted by the conversation. The need to retreat to her new home swamped her, but she did her best to shove those feelings away and continue her shopping.

When she'd finally finished and stowed everything in the back of her car, she sank into the driver's seat feeling as if she'd just run a marathon. How could one event in her life change her so much? Rob her of her energy, her true personality?

She gripped the steering wheel until her knuckles whitened. Damn Jason Garton. She wanted nothing more than to move beyond what had happened, but it looked like it was going to take more than a move to bring that to fruition.

Her phone buzzed, startling her. When she saw it was Tyler, a frisson of warmth zipped along her skin. She ran her hand back across the top of her head. How could she be so nervous around Tyler while also attracted? It was as if her old self and the one that had emerged after Jason Garton had invaded her life were dueling for primacy.

She tapped her phone's screen and read the simple response to her earlier text.

No problem.

Only two simple words, and yet she imagined hearing them in that low-timbre voice. Maybe she should take her reaction as a good sign that she was on the road back to her normal self, nothing more.

But as she drove toward the ranch, she couldn't stop hearing his voice in her head and even imagining him saying something other than the words necessary to answer her questions as his tenant. Something romantic. Something she suspected she wasn't really ready to hear, from anyone.

Chapter Four

Tyler slid his credit card through the reader on the gas pump then selected the appropriate grade. As he started filling the truck with gas, Greg Bozeman walked out of one of the auto service bays, wiping his hands on a blue shop towel.

"Hey, how's it going?" Greg asked as he approached.

"Can't complain."

"That have anything to do with your new roomie?"

"Huh?"

"Topic of the day around town is that Leah Murphy moved in out at your place."

Tyler sighed. "I rented the bunkhouse to her."

"As I recall, that's pretty close to your house."

Tyler lifted an eyebrow. "When did you become an old gossip?"

Greg's grin was full of mischief, not at all unusual for him. "Service stations are just as much a hotbed of gossip as the barbershop or the front corner of the Primrose in the mornings."

Tyler snorted. Leave it to the biggest flirt in town to know almost to the moment when a new woman moved to the county. "Don't you have a car or twelve to fix?"

"I can multitask."

Tyler shook his head as he pulled the gas nozzle from the truck's tank and replaced it back in the pump. "As far as I know, she's free, if that's what you're after."

"Not the road for me. She already turned me down. Can you believe that?"

Tyler braced his hand atop the gas pump. "Wait, you've already asked her out and she's only lived here a day?"

"Nah, it was a few months ago, when she was here visiting Conner and his family. I pulled out my best stuff, too."

A bark of laughter escaped Tyler. "And she turned you down. That's got to be a first. I don't know the woman well, but at least now I know she has taste."

"Cold, man. Cold."

Tyler laughed again as he rounded his truck. When he caught sight of Maddie coloring yet another page in the book she'd gotten at the café, he reined in his laughter.

"You must really like that coloring book."

Maddie hesitated in the strokes with the red crayon she was using before finally nodding. He went back over what he'd said, wondering how her five-year-old brain had interpreted it. Because he'd sensed concern as she'd paused in her coloring.

"That's good," he finally said, hoping to ease whatever was on her mind. "We can get you some more soon, if you'd like."

When he thought he caught a hint of a smile trying to tug at her lips, his heart lightened. He'd buy her a hundred coloring books if it would make her really smile and maybe let down her guard. Because even though she was only five, that's what was happening. For some reason, there were walls erected around his niece.

As he pulled out onto the road, she closed the coloring book and watched everything they passed the way she did every time they went anywhere. She was like a tourist in a foreign country for the first time, soaking up all the unfamiliar sights. He searched for some way to engage her in conversation but came up frustratingly empty. Instead, he let his mind wander back over the events of the day until they landed on the brief conversation with Greg, specifically the fact that Greg had asked Leah out.

He tried to imagine Leah with Greg, and he couldn't picture it. Leah seemed like a quiet person, reserved, perhaps a touch shy. Which was surprising considering her cousin was not that way. But he guessed if siblings could be like night and day, it shouldn't be a surprise if cousins were.

As he drove back toward the ranch, he wondered about his new tenant, if the situation would work out. He'd probably already made mistakes, such as not even asking what she did for a living and where she intended to work, if perhaps she already had a job before moving to Blue Falls. But really, as long as she paid her rent, didn't host wild parties and wasn't doing anything illegal, he shouldn't care. He admitted to himself he was more curious than anything.

When he pulled up beside the house a few minutes later, he saw no sign of her other than the fact her car was parked next to the bunkhouse. He supposed she was still getting settled. As he got out of his truck and Maddie released herself from her seat and headed for the house with her coloring book and crayons, he resisted the urge to go check on Leah, to see if she needed anything. He reminded himself that distance was a good thing. His number one concern was his niece, followed by his work, which meant he didn't have a lot of free time for chatting up his new neighbor.

No matter how pretty she was.

LEAH OPENED A box of beads and ran her fingers across the familiar and colorful glass, hoping a flash of inspiration would shoot up her arm to her brain. She went from box to box, knowing she had to work no matter if she felt inspired or not, but it would certainly be easier. She needed something, anything to spur her creativity.

Without thinking about it, she strolled to the window and looked toward the house. She'd heard Tyler's truck pull in a few minutes ago but saw no sign of him, the little girl or any possible wife now. But a strange pull tugged at Leah. Despite the fact that she'd been most comfortable behind locked doors since the attack, she suddenly felt as if those protective walls were closing in on her. Desperate for air, she jerked open the front door and stepped out onto the porch, leaving the door open behind her.

Despite the fact the heat of the day was still cloaking the ranch, the porch sat in the shade. She inhaled a slow, deep breath as the wave of uncharacteristic claustrophobia ebbed. A bird sang nearby, hidden somewhere in the trees across the drive. She closed her eyes and focused on the notes of its song, which found their way into her and allowed her muscles to relax and a sort of peace to soothe her. For the first time since arriving at Tyler's ranch, she thought maybe it hadn't been a mistake after all. She'd wanted peace, and this moment of connection with nature provided it.

She kept her eyes closed, afraid if she opened them the feeling would evaporate. But after several moments, the bird's song stopped. Leah opened her eyes in time to see a flash of yellow as the bird took flight. Though the bird hadn't been loud, the quiet it left behind was remarkable. As she listened, all she heard was an almost undetectable breeze rustling the leaves. The absence of traffic noise told her more than the knowledge of its distance that Houston and what had happened to her there were indeed far away.

When the air-conditioning unit for the bunkhouse clicked on, she jumped at the interruption of the quiet. Then she remembered that the front door was standing wide open, letting all the cool air outside.

Leah spun on her heel and walked back inside the bunkhouse. She actually thought she might be able to work now, but not inside. Despite the fact that the songbird had left, she found she wanted to sit outside and soak up more of what this slice of the Hill Country had to offer.

Thinking about what Gina had said earlier at the grocery, Leah selected the necessary supplies to replicate the necklace the other woman had admired. As she placed the materials around the rocking chair on the porch and took a seat, a whiff of her normal joy at immersing herself in work flirted at the edge of her mind, but was quickly gone, so quickly she actually wondered if she'd imagined it. Maybe the simple act of going through the familiar motions would lead her back to where she wanted to be.

Though she wasn't yet able to capture the usual excitement of creation, it felt good to be doing something productive. Her experience let her put together the necklace without a ton of thought. When she finally finished it, she held it up so that she could examine how it hung on the chain and make sure she hadn't made any mistakes.

Movement from down the drive drew her attention. The little blonde girl she'd seen with Tyler stood next to one of the farthest trees, about two-thirds of her body hidden behind the trunk of the red oak. When she saw that Leah had noticed her, she stepped farther out of sight.

Not wanting to scare the child, Leah didn't make any move toward her. Instead, she simply gave her a little finger wave. The girl didn't respond, instead staring for a couple of moments longer before turning and hurrying back toward the house.

Smart girl, not talking to or coming close to a stranger. Or perhaps Tyler had told her to keep her distance. Leah could totally understand that. Though she was harmless to the girl, Tyler couldn't know that. He'd barely spoken to her, knew not nearly enough about her to trust allowing his daughter to be alone with her.

Leah watched until the girl disappeared around the back of the house, then returned her attention to her work. A sense of accomplishment, that she'd taken what felt like a huge and important step in her recovery, settled in her chest. Hoping to build on that, she selected the appropriate pieces to make a set of earrings to complement the necklace. If Gina didn't want them, then Leah could always put them up for sale on her site or offer them as part of the replenishment stock for India's store.

She was midway through wrapping the wire for the second earring when her phone rang. A quick look at the display showed it was her aunt Charlotte calling. Leah exhaled, afraid she was about to be bombarded with questions despite Conner's assertion that he'd head that off at the pass. She supposed she was lucky she hadn't had to face her aunt and uncle before now.

Knowing that she couldn't avoid them now that they lived in the same town, she answered on the third ring. "Hey, Aunt Charlotte."

"Hello, dear. How are you settling in?"

"Fine. Just doing a bit of work."

"Well, hopefully you have time to spare for dinner tonight. Your uncle is grilling steaks."

Leah wasn't sure she was up to socializing yet, but then she told herself she needed to be. The quicker she resumed normal activities, the sooner she could truly get her life back and not think about what had happened all the time.

"Sounds great." Yeah, so great her stomach chose that moment to start spinning in circles.

When she hung up, she spotted Tyler striding from the house to the barn. He glanced her way and after a moment's hesitation, he lifted his hand for a single wave.

She waved back, her stomach tumbling in a very different way. How was it possible for her to feel flutters of physical attraction so soon after her attack?

That question sent awful chills racing over her skin, stinging her everywhere Garton's hands had touched her flesh.

Her peaceful afternoon shaken, she gathered up her supplies and carried them back inside. When her phone rang again, she startled and nearly dumped everything in her arms. Just the thought of hearing beads fall against the floor and spread out in all directions made nausea rise up within her.

Thinking it was her aunt again, she eased the plastic containers onto the table then pulled the phone from her shorts pocket. Instead of Charlotte, the name on the display belonged to her best friend, Reina.

Anxious to hear her friend's voice, she quickly answered before the call could go to voice mail. "Hey, there. How's the mom-to-be?"

"Fat and craving things that shouldn't be fit for human consumption."

Leah smiled. "You know you're beautiful."

Reina snorted. "That's a lie but I'll take it. But the real question is how are you? How's life in the boonies?"

"I didn't move to the Australian Outback, you know."

"Close."

Leah laughed a little, and it felt foreign and welcome at the same time. "I'm completely unpacked."

"Good, but that's not what I mean. Do you still believe it was the right decision?" Reina might tease her about her choice of new home, but she was the one person who'd supported her decision with no questions asked. She also hadn't pressed for details about the attack, knowing that Leah wasn't at a place where she could share that yet.

"It will take some getting used to, but I think so, yes."

"That's good. Maybe I'll challenge my GPS to actually find where you live once this beach ball I'm carrying decides to make an appearance."

That would mean she wouldn't see her best friend for at least another five months. "I look forward to it. Now, tell me, have you chosen a name yet?"

"Taylor and Caleb."

"Well, at least you've narrowed it down from the grocery list of names you had the last time I talked to you."

"No, that's the final names. Seems I'm having twins."

"Twins?" Leah nearly squealed. "How are you just now finding this out?"

"One of the little boogers has been hiding. If I figure out which one, he's grounded as soon as he's born."

Leah laughed again, and it filled more of her this time, reminding her of how much she'd laughed with Reina over the years.

After they talked about the babies some more and how Reina's husband, Jacob, was working more hours in order to save up for buying twice the amount of baby supplies than they'd expected, Reina shifted the topic of conversation back to Leah.

"So, tell me about your place."

"It used to be the bunkhouse on a ranch. Tyler said his father and grandfather used to have a bigger operation and their extra hands lived here."

"Tyler's your landlord?"

"Yeah."

"Good guy?"

"Conner says so. I've honestly not had much contact with him. He has a little girl, but I've not talked to her at all. Cute little thing, though."

"So this Tyler isn't some old coot wearing overalls?"

"Hardly."

The line was silent for a long moment before Reina said, "Oh?"

Leah heard the caution in her friend's voice but also the curiosity. The way she'd responded to Reina's question echoed in her head, revealing more than she'd intended, more than she'd truly realized. Despite what had happened to her and how nervous she'd been around men ever since, especially someone the size of Tyler, she couldn't deny that she found him attractive. But that didn't mean she had to go into details with her friend. More than likely, her reaction to Tyler was just a reminder that she could still be attracted to a man. Now if she could just stop being so riddled with fear around them. She had to find the appropriate level of caution that lay somewhere between fear of all men and unconcerned, but right now it felt like finding that place was as likely as her scaling Everest.

"Just because it's a small town doesn't mean everyone here is a yokel."

"I know. I just thought… Never mind. I'm glad you like it. I really do look forward to visiting you there."

"Well, for now I think you just need to take care of yourself and those babies." Leah shook her head. "Wow, two. That's kind of wild."

"Tell me about it. Though it does explain why I'm the size of a football stadium."

They talked for a few more minutes before Reina said she had to go. Leah hated to end the call but understood. She'd just tapped the end button when knocking at the door caused her to yelp and fumble her phone so much she dropped it. She picked it up then crept toward the window, her heart beating so hard she felt the pulse against her eardrums, and looked out.

Tyler stood outside with another man. When she looked closer, she realized the second man wore a uniform. Then she remembered about the internet installation. Trying to slow her heartbeat, she crossed to the door and opened it.

She managed to meet Tyler's eyes, his lovely blue eyes, and her breath caught. Then he took a step closer and the fear that was her constant companion shot up like a puck in a strong-man game at a fair. She gripped the edge of the door, ready to slam it in their faces.

But Tyler stopped moving, and his eyes narrowed a fraction as if he'd noticed her reaction and wondered at its cause. Her concern shifted directions, now causing her to worry that she'd offended the man who provided a roof over her head and a place to start over.

He gestured over his shoulder with his thumb. "Cameron is here to hook up your internet service."

Leah mustered a smile and forced her fingers to relax on the door, though she didn't release it entirely. "It's nice to meet you. Please come in." She hoped she sounded hospitable even if she felt as if she might pass out from the overload of fear coursing through her.

Cameron came inside and asked her questions

about what she'd be using the service for and told her something about download speeds. They made sense in the moment he said the words but disappeared in the next. She'd thought Tyler would leave once he'd introduced Cameron, but he didn't. Instead, he stood in the corner next to the front door, not saying anything but just…being.

Nerves of a different sort started dancing inside her. She honestly wasn't sure if she was glad he'd stayed or not. On the one hand, his presence seemed reassuring, able to easily protect her should the need arise. The height and breadth of the man were truly impressive, and a flicker of attraction tried to assert itself inside her. Honestly, it did more than try. Tyler Lowe was an attractive man. Really attractive. But he also made her feel so incredibly small and breakable.

But she was intensely aware that she was alone with two men she really didn't know, in a place where she could cry out for help in her loudest voice and never be heard.

Common sense nudged its way into her thoughts, asking how likely it was that Tyler would attack her when he had a small daughter not far away. He'd seemed to take care with the child, so that indicated he was a decent human being, right?

The cacophony of questions and concerns competing for primacy in her head made her want to scream for them all to shut up and just leave her alone.

"You okay?"

The sound of Tyler's deep voice drew her out of her thoughts.

"Uh, yeah. Just have a bit of a headache." Not exactly a lie.

Tyler's gaze left her and scanned the room. "Looks like you got settled quickly."

"Yeah, the positive side of insomnia."

"Takes a while to get used to a new place, I guess."

"Have you lived here your whole life?" What happened to keeping her distance? But it would be rude to not try to converse with him, instead standing there not even acknowledging his presence.

"Yep."

She searched frantically for an appropriate response, made more difficult by the simple fact he seemed to take up so much space. "You're lucky. It's a beautiful area."

"Yeah, it is."

They fell into a silence so awkward that she had to concentrate on not fidgeting.

"Well, I've got work to do," he said. "Let me know if you need anything."

She glanced toward him, meeting his eyes for a moment before he stepped out the door. After a few thuds of her heart, she moved to the window and watched Tyler's retreating form. As his final words before leaving replayed in her head, a crazy response coalesced in her mind. In those couple of seconds when their gazes had met, a part of her mind whispered that she wanted him to be her protector, to banish all the darkness that haunted her.

But that was weakness talking, and she needed to be strong. If she was to move beyond what happened, she had to find a way to banish the darkness and fear all on her own.

Chapter Five

Tyler walked into the cooler interior of the barn, intent on trimming the hooves on his horse, Comet. He spent so much time caring for other people's horses that he had to carve out time for the care of his own. But when he reached Comet's stall, he stopped outside and gripped the top of the stall door.

His insides were still rattled from his encounter with Leah, and he wasn't even sure why. Yes, she was pretty, but seeing a pretty woman wasn't so rare an occurrence that he should feel as if all the cells in his body were swimming around in confusion, unable to find their rightful place.

Add to that the powerful urge to protect her, and he had the crazy thought that maybe all this was an intense dream and he'd wake up and not even have a tenant in the bunkhouse.

He shook his head and scratched Comet's forehead along the white, comet-shaped blaze that had inspired the horse's name. The feeling of warm, living horse beneath his fingers told him this wasn't a dream. He really was having unexplainable reactions every time he was near Leah.

Tyler reasoned that any decent man would have

had the protective feelings when faced with the look in Leah's eyes. She'd been scared, but he couldn't figure out why. Did he scare her? Or was it Cameron? What reason had they given her to feel that way? Or was she just the nervous type, especially around men? He supposed that made sense considering how small she was, how difficult it would be to fight off unwanted advances.

He certainly hoped she didn't think he'd take advantage of her. Steering clear of any unnecessary interaction seemed more important than ever when faced with that possibility.

He retrieved his tools and got to work. Because he'd done it so many times, trimming more hooves than he could possibly remember, his thoughts drifted back to the way Greg had teased him. That was the main drawback of a small town: how people felt free to comment on or tried to steer your life the way they thought it should go. Not that Greg cared one way or the other, but there were those who did, those who would assume that a single man his age living in close proximity to a woman who looked like Leah would naturally lead to romantic involvement. He had to make sure those types of rumors didn't get started or were quashed quickly if they did. He wasn't sure what his legal status would be with Maddie if someone decided to question how fit he was to be her unofficial guardian. He didn't need anyone asking where her mother was, when she was coming back, because he had no idea. Part of him wondered if he'd ever see Kendra again.

He knew he should be sad at the possibility of never seeing his sister again, but more than anything he was angry. What kind of person abandoned her child, especially one as young and vulnerable as Maddie?

The sound of an engine starting, followed by the crunching of gravel, told him that Cameron must be finished with the internet installation. Only a few minutes went by before another engine started, indicating that Leah was leaving, as well. He couldn't help wondering where she was going. Did she get a job?

He glanced up as she drove past the entrance to the barn, and he sighed. It didn't matter where she was going. The only thing he needed to wonder about Leah Murphy was whether she would pay her rent on time. Not where she was going. Not how she spent her time at home. And not whether she was involved with anyone.

"LEAH, HONEY, CAN you help me in the kitchen?"

Leah sighed inwardly, knowing that her aunt's request probably had very little to do with her need for an extra set of hands to carry food to the table.

Why hadn't she put this gathering off a while longer? She could have claimed she was still busy getting unpacked, or too tired, or trying to finish filling an order for jewelry. As she followed her aunt into the kitchen through the French doors that led out to the patio where her uncle was grilling, she told herself she might as well get this conversation over with instead of continuing to dread it.

In fact, maybe it would be better to bring it up herself instead of letting Charlotte direct things.

"I know that Mom has probably told you what happened despite the fact that I asked her not to," Leah said as she stepped up to the marble-topped kitchen island.

"She's worried about you, dear."

"I know. And before you ask, I'm fine."

"So fine you picked up and moved."

Leah met her aunt's gaze. "I'm not going to stand here and lie to you by saying that what happened hasn't affected me, because it did. And my way of getting past it is to make some changes in my life. But I didn't move to somewhere sight unseen. You know I've always liked Blue Falls."

"But you've always lived in the city."

"And now I live in the country. Let's just leave it at that, okay?"

Charlotte pressed her lips together, as if forcibly preventing herself from asking anything else, then finally nodded once. She turned to the refrigerator and pulled out a heaping bowl of homemade mashed potatoes and then another of coleslaw.

"That looks delicious," Leah said.

"Thank you. It's nice to cook for someone besides Tom and myself."

"You mean Conner isn't over here all the time making you feed him and do his laundry?"

Charlotte laughed. "No, not usually. Even he seems to manage feeding and clothing himself."

They carried the bowls along with a basket of bread to the dining room table.

"So how is your new place really? I hear it's an old bunkhouse. That doesn't sound very homey."

"It's fine. I'm sure I'll spruce it up over time."

"You know we have perfectly good empty bedrooms here."

Her aunt meant well, but the last thing Leah wanted was a concerned family member watching her every move, reminding her through sympathetic looks that she'd been a victim of a crime, one that had shaken her to her core and filled her with a fear she'd never known before.

"I appreciate the thought, but I need my own place with plenty of room to work."

Charlotte sighed but then smiled. "Okay, but if you change your mind, you don't even have to ask. Just show up."

Conner opened the door then and held it as his dad walked in bearing a tray of perfectly grilled steaks.

They took their seats and started filling their plates. Despite the fact her aunt was probably questioning Leah's decisions as much as her parents were, thankfully her uncle didn't say anything. And Conner was Conner, sharing funny tales from work, including how an area resident called 911 convinced an intruder was trying to get into her house. When he and another deputy arrived, they found the culprit to be none other than an opossum eating the cat's food.

Conner looked at Leah. "She's one of Tyler's neighbors, so you better be on the lookout for the great possum bandit."

Leah sure hoped no critters decided to scare the living daylights out of her. She had no doubt her imagination would blow the noise way out of proportion, convincing her it was someone there to attack her.

At that thought, she glanced outside and realized it had gotten dark. "I better get going."

"It's still early," her uncle said. "Thought we might

play some cards. Been a while since we had enough people here to have a good game."

Leah smiled at her uncle. "Maybe next time. I've got a lot of work to do."

"Okay, dear. You're welcome anytime." The look in his eyes told her that he also knew what had happened to her, but at least he didn't make a big deal out of it.

"I'm going to head out, too," Conner said. "Duty calls."

"Here, let me give you some leftovers and some of this cake," Charlotte said to Leah, pointing to the four-layer chocolate cake they'd barely made a dent in.

"Don't argue," Conner said under his breath to Leah. "You'll get out of here faster."

She took his advice, but it still didn't keep her aunt from stopping her at the front door and giving her a long, tight hug.

"You remember what I said. And call me when you get home so I know you're okay."

Leah opened her mouth to reply, but Conner stepped into the conversation.

"Mom, we're not teenagers anymore. Save up all that worrying for when you have grandchildren."

Charlotte raised her brow. "And when might that be?"

"No idea. Ask your daughter."

Leah couldn't help laughing at Charlotte's eye roll.

As she and Conner walked out toward their vehicles, she said, "Nice way to throw your sister under the bus."

"What? Katie's older than me and married. The making of grandchildren is squarely in her court."

Leah snorted. "I'll be sure to tell her that the next

time I talk to her. Just remember, though, that you're here where your parents see you all the time while she's in California."

"Thanks for the reminder."

Leah reached her car and opened the driver's side door. Conner leaned his hip against the side of the car in front of her door.

"Sorry about earlier."

"About what?"

"Mom getting you alone. I hope she didn't grill you too much."

Leah shook her head. "No, it's fine. I know everyone is just concerned, trying to help. It's just something I have to get through on my own."

"So things are really okay at the new place?"

"Yeah. I got a little work done today, the first time since…"

"That's good. If you ever need anything, just let me know. Or Tyler. I'm sure he wouldn't mind helping you out with whatever you need."

"You sure about that? He seems a bit… I don't know, standoffish."

"He's just the kind of guy who minds his own business, but I don't doubt he'd give someone who needed it the shirt off his back."

"So you trust him?"

Conner looked at her, all hints of teasing gone. "I wouldn't have sent you out there if I didn't."

Leah kept repeating Conner's assertion over and over in her head as she drove toward home. It still felt weird to think of the ranch that way. The bunkhouse didn't feel like home yet, more like a temporary pit stop. But maybe that would come in time.

She navigated the last turn before she reached the driveway to the ranch. As she rounded the curve, a blur appeared across the beam of her headlights. She gasped and hit the brakes, turning to her right by instinct as her brain processed that what she was seeing was a deer. In the next fraction of a second, she realized if she didn't turn back to her left she was going to end up nose-first in the ditch. She jerked the wheel but cried out when she felt her back wheels come around and slide down the side of the road. She hit the accelerator, trying to make the back wheels gain purchase enough to get her back up on the road. In the next breath, the rear of the car slammed into something, causing the front end to slide toward the ditch. Her scream was still echoing in her head when the vehicle came to a teeth-rattling stop, the headlights illuminating the dust-filled air and part of the ditch.

Her heart beat so fast and hard that she feared it might damage itself against her rib cage. As she sat there trying to calm down, it felt as if her heart was never going to slow. But finally, it did. She took a deep breath and tried the accelerator again, hoping she could drive up onto the road. After several unsuccessful tries that did nothing more than throw up dirt and gravel along the shoulder behind her, she gave up and put the car in Park.

She let several colorful curses fly, knowing that their impetus was owed to much more than her current predicament. In an odd way, it felt good to voice her anger and frustration in such a way.

"Aahhhhhhhh!" She slammed her hands against the steering wheel, accidentally honking the horn.

Not that anyone other than some cows would hear it, or think anything of it if they did.

She pulled her phone from her purse, aiming to call Conner for help. But when she looked at the screen, she couldn't believe what she was seeing. The words *No Service* stared up at her, as if the universe was giving her a big middle finger.

"You have got to be kidding me." She dropped her head against the steering wheel, fighting tears. All she wanted was to crawl into bed and fall into a blissful, dreamless sleep. Not that she'd experienced that since before the attack.

She considered sitting in the car until someone came by, but then the thought of some man she didn't know stopping made her heart start hammering again. Maybe if she got out and walked a bit she'd pass out of the dead spot. After all, she wasn't far from the ranch and her phone worked there. Looking out at the blanket of night beyond the reach of the headlights made her want to hyperventilate.

Leah didn't know what was worse, stepping out into the night or waiting until some unknown person came by and found her alone. Deciding to act instead of sitting there working herself into an anxiety attack, she grabbed her purse in case she needed the pepper spray and got out of the car. She started walking, staring alternately at the phone screen and the inky night on the sides of the road.

"Come on, come on," she said as she walked farther and farther from the car. Still no signal.

As she started to reach the end of the area illuminated by the lights, she slowed then stopped. She looked back at her little SUV then ahead at the darkened road, weighing her options.

The sound of movement from the brush at the side of the road made her yelp. Maybe it was another deer. But when she heard what sounded like steps, panic exploded in her brain, pushing common sense completely out of her head and making her spin and start running down the road. She slipped and nearly fell, but managed to right herself before she smacked the pavement.

She imagined someone chasing her and thought maybe the panic surging through her body would kill her first, overloading her system's ability to process it. What she'd thought was a short distance to the ranch's driveway seemed to move to the edge of the earth. When she finally reached it, the night was so dark that she almost missed it. She slipped again, but this time she wasn't able to prevent the fall.

The pain shot up and down her leg as she landed hard on her hip where the pavement met the gravel drive. But she didn't give herself time to catch her breath, afraid that clasping hands were on the verge of grabbing her. She scrambled to her feet and hurried down the drive toward the ranch, each painful step bringing her closer to the relative safety of the bunkhouse. Tears won out and streaked down her face as she half ran, half hobbled through the increasingly dark night. When she finally saw the light burning in Tyler's house, she thought she'd never seen anything more wonderful. She might not know him well, but she didn't know what or who was behind her at all. And Conner trusted her safety to this man, and she trusted Conner.

She forced her pace to increase, causing her to nearly trip over her own feet. Why did the driveway seem ten times longer now than in the daylight? Her hip throbbed with every step, sending out lightning bolts of pain down her leg and up her side. The tears were joined by gasps as her lungs burned and she began to fear she wouldn't be able to make it to the bunkhouse. She couldn't stop now, not when she was so close.

Images of Jason Garton's face looming above her made a sob break free. Any moment, she expected someone to grab her and drag her to the ground, to finish what Garton had started. What if it was him? Had he gotten free and found her?

She stumbled as she reached the area next to where Tyler had parked his truck. She pitched forward onto her hands and knees, the gravel digging into her palms.

"Leah?"

She screamed and scrambled away, blinded by fear.

"What's wrong?"

A sliver of her fear parted like a curtain, allowing her to see Tyler crouched in front of her.

Instead of answering, she jerked her gaze toward the drive as it led off into the cloak of darkness. She blinked furiously, trying to clear away the tears enough that she could manage an unobstructed view. But she saw nothing. No Jason Garton. No other man intent on attacking her. Not even the cat food–stealing opossum that evidently made this area home.

"Leah, tell me what's wrong."

Not wanting to believe that she was so messed up that she'd imagined her pursuer, she was slow to shift her attention back to Tyler. But when she did, she saw genuine concern on his face. She didn't think someone could fake that so convincingly.

"I…" She swallowed and realized her throat was dry from sucking down so much late summer air. "I ran off the road."

Tyler moved closer, and she couldn't help flinching.

"Are you hurt?"

In truth, she hurt all over, but she knew he meant from the accident.

"No, but my car is still sitting on the side of the road, halfway in the westbound lane." She brought her shaking hand up to her face and shoved her hair behind her ear.

"You're bleeding."

This time Tyler didn't stop as he moved to her side. It took everything she had left within her not to flee when he touched her hand, turning it over to reveal the source of the blood was gravel scrapes on her palms.

"Come on, let's get this cleaned up."

Before she realized what he was going to do, he wrapped his arm around her shoulders and helped her to her feet. She couldn't help the wince of pain that no doubt contorted her face.

"Where else are you hurt?"

"I fell at the end of the driveway."

"Does it feel like anything is broken?"

Other than her entire life? She shook her head. "Probably just a nice bruise waiting to happen."

"Can you walk?"

That was an odd thing to ask considering she'd just come barreling onto the ranch like a crazy woman, but then she also had nearly face-planted in front of him.

"Yeah. I'm okay now." She tried to move away from him, but he didn't let her. Such an action would normally frighten her, but right now her soul cried out a thank-you for being there, supporting her.

"I've got plenty of first aid supplies in the house."

"Not necessary. I'll take care of it, but I do need to call a tow truck for my car before someone hits it."

Tyler pulled his phone from his belt and punched it a couple of times. They stood there in the dim glow coming from the house as he listened to it ring on the other end.

"Hey, Greg, it's Tyler. I need to you to come out my way as soon as you can. Leah had an accident and her car is partially in the road."

Leah managed to answer his questions about where exactly the car was and how far in the road it sat, and Greg assured them that he would be out in a few minutes. If the car was still drivable, he'd bring it to the ranch. If not, he'd take it to his shop.

"Thank you," Leah said.

"I'm just glad things weren't worse," Tyler said. "What happened?"

She shook her head. "I swerved to keep from hitting a deer and went too far and couldn't correct my mistake in time."

Tyler nodded as if he understood. "We've all had a run-in with a deer at some point or another. I ran into one last summer and had to replace the whole front grille, bumper and radiator on my truck."

Leah tried to concentrate on what he was saying, but now that the adrenaline had stopped pumping through her veins, the pain was increasing to fill the void.

"You need to get off your feet."

"I think you're right." She made to move toward her new home, but Tyler didn't let go. Instead, he supported her as she started walking, gritting her teeth so she wouldn't give voice to all the aches and stings and straight-to-the-brain pain she was feeling.

She didn't argue. Didn't have the energy, either physical or mental, to do so. While his closeness reinforced just how large he was compared with her, a sliver of rational thought told her that if he was going to hurt her, he'd have done it already. But he hadn't, instead giving her much-needed support as they made their way slowly toward the bunkhouse.

When she fumbled the keys for the front door, Tyler took them from her in a smooth motion that caused his fingers to graze the back of her hand. Despite how her body was sending out pain signals in all directions, that contact inserted a very different type of signal into the mix. For the first time since they'd met, her attraction toward him trumped the anxiety. Though she wasn't sure that was a good thing, she latched on to that feeling nonetheless. It certainly was more pleasant than the ache in her hip and the stinging across her palms.

Tyler opened the door and turned on the overhead light. "Come over to the sink."

Though he didn't touch her this time, she sensed the warmth of his hand near the small of her back as she limped toward the kitchen area. He stepped around her and turned on the cold water. Leah hesitated, anticipating that it would hurt. Tyler took her arm and gently turned her hand over and eased it under the flow. She winced at the initial contact, but relaxed as the cold gradually replaced the sting.

"Thanks for your help," she said.

"No problem. I have a lot of experience with this. My sister and I dealt with it plenty when we were growing up, usually because one of us was chasing the other."

As his words faded, she thought she detected a hint of…sorrow? But then he moved to cut off the water and dab her hands dry with paper towels.

"You have anything to put on your hands?"

She looked up at him, so close, and her breath caught on its way to give her words a voice. The realization that she was staring at him, probably with her mouth hanging open, sent a shot of "Say something, dummy!" straight to the speech center of her brain.

"Uh, yeah. Thanks for your help."

He smiled then, the first time she'd seen him smile, and it was the kind of thing that turned a reasonably intelligent woman into a blithering idiot.

"You said that already," he said.

"What?"

"You thanked me twice."

Her brain scrambled for an appropriate response, and for some reason it had her lifting her hands. "Once for each hand?"

He laughed at that, making her smile, too.

It was such a one-eighty from how she'd felt only minutes earlier as she'd fled an evidently fully imagined threat that she actually felt dizzy. And must have wobbled as a result because Tyler reached out and steadied her.

"Why don't you sit down?"

She wanted to argue that she was fine, but she wasn't sure that was true. It was as if now that she felt she was safe, her body didn't know what to do with the sudden absence of mind-numbing fear flooding through every part of her.

"I guess you're not used to having to find your way through the dark, huh?"

As Leah sat on the couch, her eyes met Tyler's. The blue reminded her of some of the glacial mountain lakes she'd seen while visiting Montana on vacation.

"Uh, no. It's really dark out there." Please don't let him ask why she was running as though an ax murderer was after her.

"Funny how the world can be so different in two places that really aren't that far apart."

"Yeah." In Houston, it was never truly dark, even in the dead of night.

She caught his gaze again, and even though he didn't say so she got the impression that he knew there was more to what had prompted her crazed race from her car to the ranch. Leah broke eye contact, partly because she didn't want to encourage more questions and partly because having him so close unnerved her. But not in a fearful way this time, at least not a fear of violence.

The sound of an engine outside drew their attention. Tyler stood and crossed to the window.

"Looks like Greg with your car."

"That was fast." She started to stand, but Tyler gestured for her to stay seated.

"I'll take care of it."

"That's not necessary. I can do it."

"I'm sure you can, but I'm already standing." He crossed to the door in two strides. "And faster than you." A hint of a smirk appeared at the edge of his mouth.

Before she could say anything, or even think of how to respond, he was out the door. And it wasn't whether her car was damaged that occupied her thoughts. Nor how she'd allowed her imagination to overwhelm her, or even how much her body hurt. Rather, her brain fixated on the man who had helped her. The feel of his strong arm around her shoulders, not allowing her to fall. The way his smile totally changed his face. And those blue eyes that drew her with a power that would scare her if she thought about it.

For tonight, she chose not to think about it.

Chapter Six

"So were you whispering sweet nothings in Leah's ear, making her drive off the side of the road?"

Tyler eyed Greg and noticed the mischief in his friend's eyes. "I wasn't even with her, you goob. She swerved to avoid a deer." He glanced at Leah's car, which didn't have any damage other than a dent where the edge of the bumper had hit the bank.

"She's lucky then," Greg said, sounding more serious.

Yeah, she was. A deer could do a lot of damage to a vehicle and the people inside. He suspected Greg was thinking over all the cars and trucks he'd hauled away from such collisions that hadn't fared so well, maybe even the occasional fatality.

"Thanks for coming out so quickly."

"Luck was with you. I'd just finished unloading a car at the station when you called." As if it were a full-moon night for towing, Greg received another call. He shook his head as he hung up. "Seems TJ put his car in the ditch again."

Tyler didn't have to ask whom Greg was talking about. Everyone in Blue Falls knew best friends TJ Malpin and Adam Parker, regular fixtures at The

Frothy Stein when they weren't sleeping it off in the drunk tank. Usually someone managed to make their car keys disappear before they could get behind the wheel and endanger anyone, but he guessed TJ was slippery tonight. And he'd bet good money that TJ wasn't getting his car or its keys back anytime soon.

He glanced toward the bunkhouse, glad it wasn't TJ's drunken driving that Leah had met out on the road.

"I'm outta here," Greg said as he opened the driver's door of the tow truck. His mischievous smile showed up even in the dim light. "Don't do anything I wouldn't do."

Tyler resisted flipping Greg the bird, but his friend must have deduced what Tyler was thinking because he was still laughing as he slipped into the truck and shut the door.

He waited until Greg was out of sight before he turned to face the bunkhouse. Before he took Leah's keys back to her, he stood and considered what had really happened before he'd seen her fall between the barn and the house. He had no doubt that she'd really run off the road to avoid a deer, but that didn't ex- plain the pure terror he'd seen on her face when he'd called out her name. Though he'd played it off as her just being unused to the deeper darkness that came from living in the country away from ever-present streetlights, something else was going on. Combined with the fact that she seemed so nervous around him, he wondered if she was running from something. Or someone. Was it something he needed to know about to ensure Maddie's safety? Maybe he should ask Conner.

His first priority was of course Maddie, but Tyler

also found himself wanting to protect Leah. Sure, he didn't really know her nor anything about her other than she was Conner's cousin, lived in Houston before coming to Blue Falls and evidently liked crafts judging by all the supplies he'd just seen on her kitchen table. But that didn't negate the feeling of protectiveness he'd experienced as he'd seen that fear in her eyes and as he'd helped her to the bunkhouse.

If he was being honest, more was at play than the urge to protect. While his main concern had been seeing her safely to the bunkhouse, he'd been aware of a warmth spreading throughout his body, originating where his arm wrapped around her small shoulders. The soft waves of her honey-blond hair had moved against his skin as they'd walked, and a faint, fruity scent had tickled his nose. Citrus of some sort.

When he'd felt her limp over the uneven ground, he'd had to resist the urge to scoop her up into his arms and carry her. He would have been able to do it so easily, but instinct told him that she was scared and doing that would have sent her over the edge.

He glanced toward the house, quiet at this hour since Maddie was asleep, then back at the bunkhouse. Maybe the buzz of attraction he'd been feeling toward Leah was a product of his mind looking for something good, something fun. He had so much worry on his mind with Kendra being MIA with her boatload of problems and Maddie barely communicating that it wasn't surprising for him to be attracted by someone beautiful and uncomplicated.

But Leah wasn't uncomplicated, was she? No, he suspected she might very well come with her own cargo hold full of baggage.

THE BIRDS CHIRPING nearby evidently didn't get the memo that it wasn't a "sing the praises of a new day" kind of morning. But then, they probably hadn't damaged themselves through irrational fear the night before either.

Leah stared at the window in her bedroom, wishing she could pull up the blinds with the power of her mind. She'd like to look out at what seemed like another beautiful morning, but the last thing she wanted to do was move. She felt as if she'd been body slammed by a professional wrestler.

That thought led to an image of Tyler in her mind. He was that big and broad, but she'd witnessed a kindness in him the night before that tempted her to get to know him better. If nothing else, it would be nice to have a friend nearby who could squash pretty much any threat that came her way. But when he'd returned to the bunkhouse with her keys after talking with Greg about her car, the distance was back, almost as if the glimpse she'd seen of the man beyond it had existed nowhere but her imagination.

Maybe it had. After all, she'd already been in full-on imagining-things-that-weren't-there mode. She closed her eyes and shook her head on the pillow. She must have looked like a deranged fool when Tyler had seen her fall. Did he think he'd made a mistake renting this place to her?

But he hadn't acted like it when he'd helped her clean the bits of gravel from her hands, although she wondered if he'd changed his mind between the time he'd left to talk to Greg and when he'd returned with her keys.

She sighed, telling herself to stop running what-if

scenarios like an Indy race in her head. If Tyler wanted her to move, she'd deal with that. And if he went back to keeping his distance, she'd roll with that, too. Right now, she needed to heave her butt out of bed and get to work. The only time in the past twenty-four hours when she'd felt almost like her old self was when she'd been sitting on the porch creating jewelry.

When she sat up on the side of the bed, she questioned her decision to move. But she forced herself to stand and head for the bathroom. As she'd expected, she was sporting quite an impressive bruise on her hip, one that felt as if it went deep. She stared at her reflection in the mirror.

"This has got to stop." *This* being the great-big fear monster that had been riding piggyback on her since that night Garton had shattered her mostly carefree existence. She wanted that back and, damn it, she was going to get it, no matter how hard it was.

After showering, dressing and eating a bowl of oatmeal, she once again carried her supplies and her cup of coffee out to the porch. Tyler's truck sat where it had the night before, but she saw no sign of him or the little girl. She wondered again if he was married, but she was leaning toward no because she doubted he would have helped her the way he had the night before if he were. At least she hoped not.

When she finished a pair of jade chandelier earrings, she looked up to stretch and noticed the little girl watching her again. This time, the child didn't hide behind a tree. But when Leah smiled and waved at her, she spun and ran back toward the house.

Leah wondered if she should ask Tyler to introduce them so that the girl wouldn't be so skittish around her, but then reconsidered. She might not be doing the girl any favors by having her trust too easily. Not that Leah had ever met Jason Garton prior to his attack on her. At least she didn't remember it. He swore to the police that she had flirted with him at the sub shop down the street from her apartment, but she had no recollection of ever even seeing him. And she was almost 100 percent certain she'd never spoken to him.

With those thoughts digging their claws into her, she found it hard to concentrate on work so carried everything back inside. Even though it was lunchtime, she'd lost her appetite. She shifted gears and worked a bit on her site and corresponding with people who'd inquired about specific items, then made an actual work plan for the rest of the week. But even all that couldn't quite dispel the toxic thoughts she'd allowed to take up residence.

Needing to move after sitting for so long, she headed outside, intent on taking a walk.

In the light of day, the expanse of the ranch seemed harmless. She examined some of the wildflowers growing across the driveway, discovering a path that led down an incline beyond the trees. Her nerves fired as she considered taking the path, fear returning at the thought of what might be lying in wait among the bushes and smaller trees.

So tired of being scared, she straightened and took a deep breath. The likelihood that someone was down there waiting for her was about as likely as her being chased by Garton through the dark the night before. "I can do this."

She eased down the path, careful not to fall again. When she rounded a bend, she spotted a creek flowing over a bed of stone. It was as if she'd stepped into a different world, one so different from the rest of the ranch that she looked behind her to see if the path still existed. Feeling a welcome peace descend on her, she walked to the water's edge and slipped off her sandals.

As she stepped into the water, she gasped at how cool it was. She looked up the creek to what looked like a low cave. Maybe the creek was spring fed, which would explain the cold water. She shifted her gaze to her feet and wiggled her toes beneath the flowing water and smiled.

She wasn't one to believe in things like fate, but she had to wonder. Her flight from Houston had been in search of a peaceful place to heal, and that journey had led her here.

Not wanting to leave, she waded for a while and skipped rocks like she had as a child when they'd visited various parks. She smiled again when she found she was still pretty good at the skipping. The longer she stayed in the little oasis, the lighter she felt. It made her wish it was visible from the bunkhouse.

After sitting on an outcropping above the creek long enough for her feet to dry, she reluctantly stood and climbed back up the path. While it felt safe to do so, she wanted to explore a bit more of her new home.

She made her way down the driveway, pausing to look out across the pasture at part of Tyler's herd of cattle. At least she thought the animals were his, but she hadn't seen him out there with them.

As she closed in on the barn area, she looked toward the house, a two-story with a mixture of limestone and pale yellow siding on the exterior. She imagined a child-sized version of Tyler and his sister growing up there with his parents. Were his parents still alive? Did his sister live in Blue Falls? She felt as if he were a mystery that would take peeling away several layers to solve.

But she wouldn't pry because she certainly didn't want to have to respond in kind. She didn't want anyone else to know about what had happened, wanted to avoid being viewed as a victim. Though if she kept acting the way she had the night before, it wasn't going to take Sherlock Holmes to figure out she was hiding something.

She pulled her gaze away from the house and wandered into the dimmer and cooler interior of the barn. She and the little girl noticed each other at the same time, startling both of them. Leah considered backing out of the barn and leaving the girl be, retreating to the bunkhouse.

But should someone this young be out here alone? Granted she didn't know what life was like for a kid growing up on a ranch, and Tyler seemed like the kind of person who'd be a protective dad. Of course, sometimes kids did things they weren't supposed to. Maybe she'd just hang out here and see if Tyler made an appearance. Where was he, anyway?

"Hi," she said, smiling.

The girl looked unsure of how or if she should respond, so Leah decided to bring herself down to her level. Looking to the side of the barn's main alley, she spotted some square hay bales and sank onto one of the stacks, unable to prevent a wince and groan.

The little girl gripped a slat in one of the horse stalls. "Are you hurt?"

Her little voice was so sweet sounding, small and concerned but also a touch timid.

"I fell down last night, and I'm a bit sore today."

The girl just stared at her with big blue eyes that looked a lot like Tyler's.

"I'm Leah. I'm the one who moved into the bunkhouse." Leah didn't push the girl to give her any information if she didn't want to, instead glancing over to where a beautiful brown horse was sticking his head over the stall door above the child. He seemed to be smelling the girl's hair. His nose must have made contact and tickled because the girl giggled.

The sound was so full of innocence and childlike joy that, combined with the lovely creek she'd found, Leah was able to experience a moment of joy of her own. It felt good to be moving closer to the person she was at her core—outgoing, friendly, able to enjoy life to the fullest.

The girl reached up and rubbed the horse's nose with a tenderness that touched Leah's heart. She'd not thought much about having her own children despite her mother's less-than-subtle hints about grandchildren. Though her mom and Charlotte were related only by virtue of marrying brothers, they were very much alike in that department. As Leah watched the little girl in front of her, however, she thought maybe someday it would be nice to have a child so cute and sweet.

As if the girl sensed Leah watching her, she met her gaze. For a moment her forehead scrunched, but then she said, "My name is Maddie."

"It's nice to meet you, Maddie. It seems you have quite the friend there."

"His name is Comet, because of his forehead."

Leah noted the white area running the length of the horse's head, larger at the top and trailing to end right above his nose. Comet seemed an appropriate name.

"What do you do on the porch every day?"

Leah shifted her attention back to Maddie. "I make jewelry. That's my job, making necklaces, bracelets and earrings and selling them to people."

"Cool." Maddie fiddled with the bottom of her T-shirt, which had a glittery pony on it. She seemed to be thinking hard about something, judging from the way her forehead wrinkled. After a few seconds, she met Leah's eyes again. "Could I watch you?"

"Sure, if you have permission to come up to the bunkhouse."

Maddie looked confused for a moment then looked past Leah toward the house.

Leah glanced over her shoulder, wondering why Maddie seemed so concerned. Did she think her father wouldn't allow her to watch Leah work? Was Tyler strict with the girl? Was that why she seemed so shy and withdrawn? A wave of protectiveness washed over Leah. Maddie was so small and vulnerable. Tyler seemed like a good guy, but what if his parenting style instilled fear in his daughter?

She tried to remind herself that it wasn't her business. Maddie didn't have any outward signs of abuse, so maybe Leah was worrying for no reason. That seemed to be commonplace lately, after all.

"Would you like me to ask for you?"

Maddie shook her head, and Leah decided to let Maddie take care of the request herself. She just hoped Tyler wouldn't refuse her.

"Well, I'm going to be working on the porch this afternoon if you want to come up and watch."

"Okay. Thank you." The politeness, almost sounding formal, made Leah smile.

"You're welcome. It'll be nice to have company." Cute, sweet, harmless company. Maddie seemed interested and Leah thought maybe it would be another way to keep her own thoughts on something other than what she'd run from.

As the afternoon progressed with no sign of Maddie, Leah wondered if Tyler had said no to her request or if Maddie hadn't asked. She considered walking down to the barn, where she could hear the occasional ring of metal, probably Tyler shoeing the horse that had been unloaded from a trailer earlier, and asking on Maddie's behalf. But would he see that as a virtual stranger butting her nose into his private business? They'd had a pleasant exchange the night before, and she didn't want to risk damaging that fledgling friendship, if that's what it was.

She took a break to go to the bathroom then trade out her completed pieces for new supplies for her next project. When she returned to the porch, Maddie was standing at the edge of the drive in front of the bunkhouse. Leah smiled and gestured for her to come closer.

"Have a seat, sweetie. I'm starting a new necklace. I think you'll like this one." Leah pulled out her bead board and started lining up the chunky gumball beads she'd selected in pink, pearl, black and silver. She tilted the board slightly so Maddie could see from where she'd seated herself on the edge of the porch. "I decide how long I want the necklace to be and measure it out on this board. Then I line up the beads in the right order."

Leah shifted some of the beads so she could insert a few pink rose-shaped beads.

"Those are pretty," Maddie said.

"I thought you might like them." As Leah worked, she explained each step in the process. Every time she glanced up, Maddie was paying such close attention that the world around her had seemed to fade away.

"So, how old are you, Miss Maddie?"

"Five."

"Five, that's a good age."

"How old are you?"

Leah chuckled. "A lot older than five. How old do you think I am?"

Maddie shrugged.

Leah leaned forward, as if sharing a secret. "Twenty-nine."

Maddie's eyes widened, as if twenty-nine were ancient. It probably was to a five-year-old.

Leah laughed. "That's probably not much different than your dad's age."

Confusion filled Maddie's face again. Maybe she had no idea how old her dad was. It was probably a bit like thinking about your parents by their first names.

The sound of crunching gravel drew Leah's attention at the same time that Maddie spun toward the sound. Again, Leah wondered about Tyler's parenting style when Maddie's body stiffened, as if she expected to be punished.

"Maddie, I didn't know where you'd gotten off to."

Even though his voice was full of concern instead

of anger, Maddie still appeared as though she might run away from him at any moment.

"I'm sorry," Maddie said in a voice so small it broke Leah's heart.

"I was just showing Maddie how I make jewelry. We've been having a nice afternoon. We met in the barn earlier and I told her she was welcome to watch anytime. I hope that's okay." Leah suspected that Maddie hadn't asked for permission, but she didn't want to see her get into trouble.

Tyler eyed Maddie. "It's okay. I just couldn't find her and got worried."

Maddie looked at Leah, and there in her eyes was the admission that she hadn't asked Tyler for permission. Nonetheless, Leah smiled at her, hoping to ease some of her obvious anxiety.

When Tyler moved toward the porch, Maddie eased to her feet. She met Leah's gaze again. "Thank you."

"You're welcome, sweetie." She wanted to invite Maddie back again, but she needed to clear it with Tyler. Maybe she should have done that in the first place.

Without looking at Tyler, Maddie hurried down the driveway toward the house.

Leah watched the little girl, curious what was running through her head. When she shifted her gaze to Tyler, she was surprised to see a raw expression of helplessness. Again, Leah wondered where Leah's mother was. A horrible thought occurred to her, that perhaps the woman had died and Tyler and Maddie were still in mourning.

"I hope Maddie wasn't bothering you," he said as he looked her way.

"Not at all. I was happy to have the company. You have a lovely daughter."

He shook his head, glancing down the driveway to where Maddie was now climbing the front steps of the house.

"She's my niece."

Niece? She recalled him mentioning his sister, but she hadn't gotten the impression that she was no longer alive. Maybe Maddie was just here for a visit?

Tyler started to step away from the porch, but something compelled Leah to stop him. Maybe it was another part of her old self reemerging, the part that liked connection with others and helping out when she could.

"Is something wrong?"

Tyler hesitated for a moment. "Nothing I can't handle."

As he walked away, Leah wasn't so sure about that.

Chapter Seven

Tyler's heart rate had finally slowed by the time he returned to the house. When he hadn't been able to find Maddie in the barn or the house, he'd been scared out of his mind. When he'd finally thought about the bunkhouse, he'd spotted her almost immediately, her little purple shirt bright against the predominant browns and greens of the ranch. His first instinct had been to scold her for running off without telling him, but instinct told him that wasn't wise. She was already so skittish that he didn't want to add to whatever reason she had for being that way. He would just be glad she was okay and that Leah didn't seem to mind hanging out with a five-year-old.

He climbed the front steps and took a deep breath before going inside. He considered going up to Maddie's room to talk to her, but decided he'd make dinner first and they could talk over their meal. That was if Maddie would talk. He wondered for what felt like the millionth time why his niece was so quiet, why she'd changed so much from when she was a toddler.

When he finished cooking and set the food on the table, he called Maddie downstairs to eat. Not only was she quiet, but she wouldn't even meet his eyes.

"Honey, I'm not mad at you, if that's what you think. I was just worried because I didn't know where you were. Why did you go up to Leah's without telling me?"

She shrugged her little shoulders.

A part of him filled with an extra well of frustration. For some reason, Maddie had sought out a stranger to talk to instead of him. But if that would help her come out of her shell, he had to allow it and not let his own feelings get in the way.

"If Leah doesn't mind, you can go up there to visit. Just always ask if it's okay with her."

Maddie nodded.

He ached to say more, to beg her to open up and talk to him, but he kept himself in check. His gut told him baby steps were the key to connecting with his niece again.

After they finished eating, Maddie asked to be excused. Though he really wanted her to stay and talk, he was too tired to figure out a new tactic. So he consented and she headed off to color or watch cartoons or whatever she had planned for her little girl evening.

Tyler couldn't sit still, didn't even take the time to clear the dishes from the table. He stalked outside and kept walking down the driveway. He wanted to scream at Kendra for abandoning her child, for whatever she'd done to make Maddie so withdrawn. How had his sister gotten so messed up? He wondered yet again if there had been anything he could have done to prevent it. Though he missed his parents, a part of him was glad they weren't around to see what had become of their only daughter.

As he walked back toward the house, he spotted

a light shining in the bunkhouse. He had the oddest urge to go sit on Leah's porch with her the way Maddie had. But the last person he should be sharing his family drama with was a woman he'd met only a few days before. Even if doing exactly that tempted him like nothing had in a long time.

TYLER MUST HAVE given Maddie his okay to visit her because over the next three days, Maddie made an appearance on Leah's front porch. They chatted about the ranch, Maddie's favorite colors and the little stuffed puppy that Maddie often had with her. Leah found out the puppy's name was Daisy and was Maddie's best friend.

She'd gathered that Maddie was an only child. Being one herself, Leah understood the need to have a special friend.

"I had a stuffed bunny when I was a little girl. His name was Fluffy. Not too original, but he was my best friend, too."

"Do you still have him?"

"No. When I grew up, he went to live with another little girl." Okay, maybe that was a white lie. But even though she was pretty sure Fluffy ended up being donated to a thrift store, she found she liked the idea of him being a special friend to some other kid.

Maddie played with Daisy for a couple of minutes before shifting her gaze back to Leah. "Do you have brothers and sisters?"

"No, I'm an only child."

"Like me."

"Yes."

"Is your mom gone, too?"

Gone? What exactly did Maddie mean by that? Leah swallowed, trying to figure out how best to respond.

"No. She and my dad live in Houston. I used to live there, too, until I moved here."

"My mom didn't want me anymore."

Leah's heart ached at the mixture of sadness and acceptance in Maddie's voice.

"What do you mean, honey?"

"She left with her boyfriend."

Had Maddie somehow construed her mom leaving Maddie with her uncle while her mother went on a vacation with her boyfriend as being abandoned? How long had she been gone anyway? Not wanting to upset Maddie any more, Leah didn't ask her anything more about her mom.

"Your uncle Tyler seems like a nice guy."

Maddie didn't immediately reply, but after a couple of moments she nodded once.

Left not knowing what to say next, Leah was glad for the project she was just completing. "Maddie, can you come try this on? I want to see what it looks like on someone."

Maddie got to her feet and crossed to Leah with less hesitance than she'd expected. Maddie extended her arm, and Leah slid the bracelet made from alternating pink and purple cat's-eye beads onto Maddie's wrist.

"It's pretty. I like pink and purple."

Leah smiled. "I'm glad you like it because I made it for you."

Maddie's eyes widened and her mouth dropped open a little. "For me?"

Leah nodded then pointed toward the silver-plated "M" that coexisted with the string of beads. "See, that's for 'Maddie'."

Maddie ran the fingers of her other hand over the beads then along the shape of the "M" before suddenly wrapping her arms around Leah's neck.

Tears stung Leah's eyes, her heart filling with happiness that something as simple as a bracelet had made this little girl happy.

Beyond Maddie, Leah saw movement that turned out to be Tyler. He was staring at them as if he couldn't believe what he was seeing.

"Hi, Tyler," Leah said as Maddie released her. She sensed that some part of Maddie wanted to share what she'd received with him. She lightly squeezed Maddie's hand. "Why don't you show your uncle your new bracelet?"

As if given a boost of courage, Maddie moved to the edge of the porch and extended her arm.

"Leah made it for me."

The smile on Tyler's face added to the full feeling in Leah's heart.

"That was nice of her," Tyler said, then looked beyond Maddie to Leah. He nodded in thanks.

"It was nothing. Maddie has been good company, helping me settle in."

In that moment, Leah realized that she wasn't just saying the words. The past few mornings she'd actually gotten up with a purpose for her days. Maddie might be only five, but Leah enjoyed spending time with her. And she'd made more jewelry in the past few days than she had in all the other time since the attack.

She still wasn't comfortable enough to step outside at night and hadn't gotten past jumping at every sound, but she had to believe that would come in time. After all, things were already better than when she'd first arrived on the ranch.

Despite how happy Maddie seemed now, Leah couldn't forget what she'd said about her mother. She wanted to ask Tyler about it, but not with Maddie within earshot. Maybe it was good the opportunity didn't present itself because, really, it wasn't any of Leah's business, no matter how protective she felt about Maddie after so little time of knowing her.

"Well, squirt, we need to head out. I've got one more job to do today."

Maddie glanced back at Leah, but Leah didn't feel she could offer to let Maddie stay with her. Having her watch her work within full view of the house and barn was one thing, but Tyler leaving his niece with an almost complete stranger was quite another.

"I bet you see lots of pretty horses going with your uncle," she said instead. "Who knows, maybe you'll work with animals when you grow up."

"Or make jewelry."

Leah smiled. "Or maybe both."

As Tyler and Maddie headed down the driveway, Leah noticed that Maddie didn't reach for her uncle's hand. It could just be the girl's independence asserting itself, but something didn't sit right with Leah. Her gut told her that Tyler was a good guy and would never hurt Maddie, but something was going on. She couldn't stop thinking about it as she started on another necklace-and-earring combo. Maddie's words about her mother echoed in Leah's head while she gathered up her supplies as the sun neared the horizon, and followed her as she went inside to make a sandwich.

When a stronger breeze started rustling the leaves on the oaks, she took her sandwich and lemonade outside to enjoy the sunset and slightly cooler temperature. As she was taking her last bite, she heard what she'd come to recognize as the sound of Tyler's truck. She watched as he and Maddie carried grocery bags inside the house. The ongoing internal debate about whether she should mention to Tyler what Maddie had said didn't show any signs of quieting.

By the time she saw Tyler come back out and head toward the barn, she realized she wasn't going to be able to rest until she talked to Tyler. She took a deep breath, trying not to think that she was about to butt her nose into the family business of a man big enough to break her in two, and got to her feet.

When she reached the barn, Tyler was already busy cleaning out Comet's stall. When he saw her, he stopped what he was doing.

"Can I help you with something?" he asked.

She hesitated, considering making up some story about why she was in the barn other than the real reason. But she'd come this far.

"I apologize in advance if this comes across as me being too nosy, but I wanted to make you aware of something Maddie told me today. I know sometimes kids can misinterpret things."

"Okay." He said the single word slowly, as if he wasn't sure if he wanted to hear what she had to say.

Leah swallowed and shoved her hands into the pockets of her cargo capris. "She said her mother didn't want her anymore. And the way she said it just broke my heart."

At first Tyler didn't say anything, but the way he was gripping the handle of the rake, as if choking the life out of it, lit a fire under Leah's easy panic. Without even thinking about it, she took a step backward.

"Kendra has problems, and she left Maddie with me."

Tyler sounded as if sadness was trying to hollow him out to make more room for itself. Something inside Leah responded to that, wanting to help him as much as she did Maddie. The fear of Tyler and what he could do to her ebbed, and she crossed to the outside of the stall.

"Has she been here long?"

"A few weeks." He leaned the rake against the side of the stall but then looked like a boat adrift at sea without it. "Maddie didn't used to be so quiet and withdrawn, but I hadn't seen her much in the past couple of years. My sister was always drifting from one place to another, so sometimes I didn't even know where they were."

Leah was surprised Tyler was sharing so much, but she got the feeling it had been bottled up and festering since his sister had left Maddie with him.

"Is she an addict?"

His gaze came up to meet hers, seemingly surprised she'd come to that conclusion so easily. "Yes."

"My best friend's brother went through a really dark period with drug addiction, but he eventually got help and is doing much better now."

The sadness in Tyler's eyes yanked on her heartstrings.

"Kendra doesn't want to be helped. Any time I've suggested it, she's told me exactly where I can go."

"But she must trust you or she wouldn't have left her daughter with you."

Tyler took off his hat and ran his fingers back through his hair. "More likely she's burned all her bridges and she knew I wouldn't refuse. Not that I had much time to do so. She barely stopped the car long enough to drop Maddie off." He laughed, but it held no humor. "Her latest loser of a boyfriend didn't even turn off the car's engine."

"I'm sorry. I know all of this must be hard for you. I hope I haven't added to that."

"Not at all." He braced one tanned, muscled arm against the top of the stall next to the door. "Maddie has actually spoken a bit more since she started coming up to watch you work."

"I'm glad if I was able to help in some way. She's a sweet girl."

An awkward silence descended between them.

"So that's what you do for a living, make jewelry?"

Was he worried that she wouldn't be able to pay the rent?

She nodded. "I sell through an online store and in various shops, like India Parrish's in town."

"Ah." He nodded in acknowledgment.

Before the awkward silence could insert itself again, she said, "Speaking of, I better get back to it." She turned to leave.

"Leah."

She really liked the way her name sounded when he said it, more than she should. But it was unreasonable to expect her to not react to that deep, rumbling voice.

"Thanks for telling me about Maddie."

"You're welcome. I'm just glad you don't think I overstepped."

"I hope you don't think I overshared."

She smiled. "Sometimes it's easier to talk to someone you don't really know."

"Yeah."

As Leah walked back to the bunkhouse, she felt better than she had in weeks. Maybe the key to helping herself was to focus on helping others. She glanced back toward the barn, wondering how she might be able to help Tyler.

She swore to herself it had nothing to do with how good-looking he was, how he stirred a buzzy awareness in her despite what she'd been through. As she stepped inside, she wondered if she was lying to herself.

Chapter Eight

Tyler shook Avery Potter's hand. "Thanks for your time."

"That's why I'm here." Then the kindergarten teacher squatted down in front of Maddie. "I'm looking forward to having you in my class."

"Will we color?"

It was only three simple words, but Tyler rejoiced at hearing his niece say anything. If only she'd talk to him other than to answer direct questions. The fact that she'd told Leah about her mother abandoning her still weighed on him, had kept him from sleeping more than a couple of hours the night before.

Avery smiled. "Yes, we will. And we'll learn lots of really fun stuff. I'll see you on Monday, okay?"

Maddie nodded. "Okay."

As they walked down the corridor toward the exit, Tyler noticed Maddie eyeing the other kids near her age walking up and down the hallway with their parents. He wondered if she felt strange being there with him or if it would be strange even if she were with Kendra.

He did his best to tamp down the simmering anger at his sister. He'd tried again that morning to reach her, but he'd still received no response. How could she just disappear and not even check on her child? Leah, a woman who barely even knew Maddie, showed more concern.

Tyler held the heavy door at the exit while Maddie walked through. "What do you say we go get your school supplies?"

"Okay."

Was there less hesitation before she answered him, or did he imagine it?

When they reached the store, he pulled out the school supply list. "I'll read things on the list and you pick out the ones you want, okay?"

Maddie actually looked up at him, met his eyes, something she hadn't done much since arriving on his doorstep. Evidently deciding he wasn't pulling her leg, she made for a mixture of supplies decorated with everything from puppies to princesses as he read the list. He honestly didn't even look at the prices. If she wanted the most expensive princess backpack, then that's what she would get. He didn't think kids should always be spoiled with the most expensive options available, but for now he felt Maddie needed to know that he cared about her, that he wanted her to be happy. She was going to go to school for the first time, which was scary enough, but it was where she didn't have any friends. Hell, he didn't even know if Kendra stayed in one place long enough for Maddie to have friends anywhere.

For the first time, he considered what he would do if Kendra deigned to show up for Maddie. He wasn't sure he'd be willing to give her back. The last thing a child needed was a strung out parent with questionable decision-making abilities.

When they completed checking everything off the list, Tyler spotted Maddie glancing at the coloring books, almost as if she was afraid to ask if she could have one.

"Would you like some new coloring books?"

She eyed the books again then looked up at him. "Is that okay?" Her voice sounded impossibly small.

"Of course, honey. Go ahead." He motioned toward the books, and Maddie walked over and went from one book to the next, seeming to carefully consider her options.

Finally, she chose one about baby animals. She handled the book so carefully that it made him wonder if Kendra, in addition to probably being an unfit mother, had denied her only child simple pleasures. His heart aching for both Maddie and for the little girl Kendra had once been, he stepped up to the shelves and selected four more coloring books and the biggest box of crayons they had. When he put them in the cart, Maddie looked up at him with confusion knitting her brows.

"I can only have one."

"Why do you say that?" Although he was pretty sure he already knew the answer.

"Mom said."

"But I'm not your mom. Uncles get to buy presents for their nieces." Unable to keep his distance any longer, he gently smoothed her silky blond hair. He counted it a big victory that she let him.

As they walked toward the cash register, Maddie still looked wary, as if she thought he might suddenly change his mind and put everything back. But as he placed the items on the conveyor belt for the cashier to ring up, her eyes lit up with an excitement he hadn't seen since she was a toddler. If what he was buying had cost ten times what it did, it would be worth every penny.

When he had the supplies and Maddie loaded into the truck, he looked across the cab at her. "All this shopping has made me hungry for a treat. I think we should go to the bakery. Would you like that?"

She smiled a little and nodded. His heart lifted at the sight.

A few minutes later, they walked into the Mehlerhaus Bakcry to see that both Keri and her sister-in-law Josephina were working.

"Well, hey there," Keri said. "That's quite the pretty little lady accompanying you today."

"Maddie, this is Keri. She owns the bakery. And Josephina. They make all the things you see here."

"Hello," Maddie said, looking up at even more new faces.

"It's nice to meet you, Maddie," Keri said.

Josephina moved behind the glass display case. "What looks good to you?"

His niece took a couple of steps until she was mere inches from the glass. Again, she took her time considering before pointing toward a cookie decorated with pink and white icing.

"Excellent choice," Josephina said, then met Tyler's gaze. "And for you?"

"I'll take an oatmeal raisin cookie."

As he moved toward the cash register, he felt Maddie's small hand barely touch his arm. "Did you want something else?"

"Can we get Leah a cookie?"

Tyler noticed how the two women responded to Maddie's question, with a bit more interest than he liked. Again thinking of his iffy situation with Maddie, he didn't want anyone thinking anything inappropriate was going on at the ranch.

"Sure. Go ahead and pick out a couple." When Maddie moved back to the glass case, he pulled out his wallet. As Josephina helped Maddie, Keri stepped up to the register. "Leah's been showing Maddie how to make jewelry."

"Oh, that's nice of her. Leah makes beautiful stuff."

"She made me this," Maddie said as she lifted up her arm to show off the bracelet Leah had gifted her.

"That's very pretty, just like you." Keri shifted her gaze back to Tyler. "And Leah."

He didn't respond. It was a no-win situation. If he agreed, Keri might read more into it than was there. Even if he might admit to himself that he'd been thinking of Leah more than he ought to. But if he disagreed with Keri, she'd for sure know he was hiding something because no man in his right mind would think Leah was unattractive. Even when she'd been hobbling, injured, her hands bleeding, she'd been beautiful. Disheveled and definitely afraid of something, but beautiful nonetheless.

After he paid for the cookies and Keri gave back his change, he directed Maddie toward the door.

"Come back soon. And bring Leah with you next time."

As he stepped out onto the sidewalk, he wondered if town matchmaker Verona Charles had started recruiting assistants in her shenanigans.

WHEN THEY RETURNED to the ranch, Leah wasn't sitting out on her porch. Tyler tried to ignore the pang of disappointment he felt. In such a short time, he'd gotten used to seeing her there. Even though she wasn't a part of his family, hadn't even been remotely a part of his life for long, he somehow felt less alone with her living nearby. Hell, he hadn't even realized he felt alone, probably hadn't until Kendra had left Maddie with him and he had to stumble his way through being a pseudo-parent.

He started toward the house, but was shocked when Maddie grabbed his hand. She held up the bag she'd kept close since they left the bakery.

"Can I take Leah her cookies?"

"She's not outside, so she might not want company right now."

The crestfallen look on Maddie's face made him afraid she'd retreat back into her shell of silence again.

"But we can go check."

Maddie was capable of making her own way up to the bunkhouse, but he didn't want to let go of her hand quite yet. A lump formed in his throat at a sudden memory of holding Kendra's hand as they walked to the school bus at the end of the driveway. She'd looked up to him then. Sometime in the intervening years, she'd stopped.

As he accompanied Maddie up the driveway, he admitted to himself that he also wanted to see Leah. Her smile made him believe everything was going to turn out all right, which of course was a crazy thought considering nothing Leah did or said would make Kendra not a screwed-up junkie. Still, something about her lessened the weight pressing down on him, if only for a few minutes.

A strange jitteriness started in his middle as he

reached up to knock on the door. When he got no response, he thought maybe Leah had gone for a walk. He looked in both directions but didn't see her. Had she gone down to the creek? But then he heard a yelp from inside, sending him barreling inside before he could think better of it.

"Leah?"

"Tyler? Could use a little help here."

He headed toward the utility room, trying to determine the source of the hissing sound. He realized what it was right before he reached the open door. Inside, Leah was tossing towels on top of the water heater, which was spraying water all over the room. Leah was completely drenched, her hair flattened and dripping, her feet sloshing in the water puddling on the floor.

He pushed past her to the water cut off and twisted it. The spray stopped, but the water heater was obviously toast.

"I'm sorry," Leah said. "I started a load of laundry and left the room. When I came back, this was in full swing." She gestured around her, water dropping off her fingertips.

Tyler did his best not to stare at where her T-shirt was plastered to her breasts. So he forced his gaze upward and saw how bedraggled she looked. Before he could stop it, a snort of laughter came out.

Leah stared at him, openmouthed. "Are you laughing at me?"

"Yes. Yes, I am."

She started to say something, but in the next moment she was laughing, too. "I bet I'm a sight."

"A little on the wet side."

"Like I just walked out of the lake." She looked around her. "Good grief, what a mess."

"We'll get this cleaned up in no time."

With Leah mopping, Tyler disconnecting and hauling out the old water heater, and even Maddie helping in small ways like opening a door or bringing Leah a roll of paper towels, they did finish in a surprisingly short amount of time. Leah opened the windows and Tyler brought in a large fan to finish drying out the room.

"We make a pretty good team," he said. It was strange how natural it felt for the three of them to work together.

"Yeah, we do. But this member of the team needs to change into dry clothes."

"I won't be able to get a new water heater until at least tomorrow, so you can finish your laundry and clean up down at the house."

Leah met his gaze, and he saw indecision and maybe a layer of unease in her eyes.

"I don't want to impose."

"It's not imposing if I invite you."

"Um, okay then."

"I brought you cookies," Maddie said out of the blue. She held up the bakery bag.

"You did? That was nice of you." Leah took the bag and looked inside. "These look yummy. Can you hold on to them for me until we get down to the house?"

Maddie nodded.

When Tyler held open the door of his house for Leah a few minutes later, the jitters made a reappearance in his stomach.

Come on, get a grip.

He waited for Maddie to step inside, too, then entered, closing the door behind him.

"The laundry room is this way," he said, leading the way into the kitchen, then pointing at the door on the opposite side of the room. "And if you want to take a shower, you can use the bathroom at the top of the stairs."

Leah glanced toward him. She smiled, but there was definitely a touch of wariness about it. A wariness he very much wanted to erase.

LEAH'S MIND BALKED at the side of the kitchen nearest the front door, her closest route of escape. Did she dare step farther into Tyler's house?

She did her best to keep her fearful imagination from galloping off like a runaway horse as it had the night she'd almost hit the deer. Tyler had given her no reason to suspect he would hurt her. Quite the opposite. All her interactions with him spun through her head like highlight clips from a movie—

How he'd helped her the night she'd injured herself, his confession about his sister, the gentle way he had with Maddie, helping her with the flooding caused by the busted water heater.

The truth was if she wanted to get past the attack, she had to learn to trust again. To not see potential danger in everyone with a Y chromosome.

"Thank you," she finally said and carried her laundry to the room he'd indicated. She wondered if she'd telegraphed her fear because Tyler stayed on the opposite side of kitchen, not crowding her in the small laundry room.

If she was going to take a shower—and she could

use one considering her current state—she needed to wait to start her laundry. She grabbed her clean clothes and retraced her steps.

She offered Tyler a small smile as she passed back through the kitchen on the way to the stairs and hoped it didn't reveal how nervous she was to be here.

Maddie met her at the top of the stairs, a folded white towel in her hands. She provided a blessed distraction, allowing the spinning in Leah's head to slow.

"You can use my shampoo," Maddie said. "It's in the shower."

"Thank you, sweetie." She gently gripped the little girl's shoulder for a moment before heading into the bathroom.

Once inside, she locked the door and stared at her bedraggled appearance in the mirror. Wow, she certainly was a sight, and not a pretty one. Her hair was plastered to her head like seaweed, and her clothing didn't look much better. She listened to the sounds of Tyler moving around downstairs and shivered at the idea of even taking off her clothes under the same roof. And for a moment, she wondered if part of the reason had nothing to do with her attack. The spinning started up again, this time in her stomach. She pressed her hand against her middle as if that would somehow stop it.

Her feelings toward Tyler felt like strands of spaghetti all twisted together. He was a man, a big one, and so the frightened part of her still worried he posed a threat. But she suspected that was simply a posttraumatic reaction, the primal need for survival trying to usurp her common sense, which was telling her he wouldn't hurt her. Mixed up with all that was the fact

that every day she seemed to think about him more—
those glacial blue eyes, the tender way he'd held her
the night she'd fallen despite how much brute strength
he no doubt had at his disposal, the way his smile
seemed to erase all the worry she saw him carrying
around like an invisible sack of grain on his back.

If she could just take off her clothes, step into that
shower, it'd be another important step on the road to
her recovery. She continued to stare at herself in the
mirror for at least another minute while the argument
between her two halves continued in her head.

"Just stop it," she hissed at herself, then yanked
her T-shirt over her head and dropped it with a damp
splat on the floor.

When she stepped under the warm flow of water,
she reached for the bottle of shampoo on the side of
the tub. She expected a bottle decorated by some car-
toon character. Instead, it was regular shampoo that
didn't smell remotely girlie at all. In fact, she suspected it was an extra bottle of the kind she'd find in
Tyler's bathroom. She didn't know whether to laugh
or cry at that realization.

It drove home, strangely more than anything else,
that she wasn't the only person in the world dealing
with hard times. Yes, her skin still crawled every time
she thought of that night, of Garton's hands on her,
but it could have been worse. He hadn't killed her. He
hadn't raped her.

She had parents who loved her, had always been
there for her. Conner had helped her without hesitation, and she knew her aunt and uncle cared about her
welfare, too. She couldn't fathom her own mother not
wanting her anymore, leaving her without a backward

glance. And she couldn't imagine suddenly being thrust into the parenting role for a traumatized child with no one to help.

Leah realized tears were mixing with the water from the shower. Her heart ached for Maddie and for Tyler. She wished there was something she could do to help them other than simply spending a bit of time with Maddie.

She stayed in the shower longer than she should have, but she wanted evidence of her crying to fade before she went back downstairs. How would she explain red, puffy eyes? A busted water heater didn't seem like a plausible, sane reason. Crying over their situation seemed perhaps too much, too soon. And she certainly didn't plan to share her own story. She didn't want to see the look in Tyler's eyes she'd seen in her mother's: that suddenly Leah was a fragile little bird who had to be handled with a delicate hand.

After she was finished in the bathroom, Leah headed toward the stairs. As she reached them, she glanced to her left and saw Maddie in her room having a conversation with her stuffed puppy. She was so engrossed that she didn't notice Leah. Captivated by the pure innocence of the scene, Leah couldn't help watching for a bit longer.

Something made Maddie look up. When she saw Leah, she smiled, hopped to her feet and stepped out into the hall, bringing her puppy with her.

"Do you want your cookies now?"

Leah returned her smile. "That sounds good."

Maddie led the way down the stairs, holding on to the handrail with one hand and clutching her puppy with the other. As Leah watched Maddie, it was strange to think she had been that small once. She tried to remember what the world had looked like to her at that age and couldn't.

After Leah took a minute to start her load of wet laundry, she returned to the kitchen just as Tyler was getting off the phone.

"Good news," he said. "I can get a new water heater tomorrow, the last one they have at the hardware in town."

"I'm sorry to add to your workload."

"No need to apologize. Water heaters die." He glanced toward the laundry room door, which she'd closed to keep out the noise. "Since you've got to wait for your clothes, how about some dinner?"

"Tyler, I can go back to the bunkhouse and eat, then come back for my laundry."

"But you have to eat your cookies," Maddie said, sounding worried, as though Leah had forgotten.

Tyler smiled as he looked at his niece, a look so full of love that Leah's admiration of him seemed to grow tenfold in the space of a single heartbeat.

"There is that." Tyler looked at Leah, trying but failing to hide a smile, one that said he was confident he'd win this mini war. "You could have the cookies as dessert, after dinner."

Though Maddie didn't say anything, Leah could tell from the girl's hopeful expression that she wanted her to stay, as well.

"Okay, but you have to let me help."

"Deal."

The way Tyler looked at her before he turned to open the refrigerator made giddy little bubbles pop throughout Leah's body. She forced herself to take a deep breath, quietly, before she moved to help him prepare dinner.

By the time she tossed her laundry into the dryer, they were ready to sit down to a meal of pork chops, green beans and salad. As Leah filled her plate, she searched for a topic of conversation.

"So, Maddie, I didn't see you earlier today. What were you and your uncle up to?"

"We went to school and then bought stuff for school, and coloring books and crayons."

"That does sound like a busy day. School, huh?"

"Yes, Miss Maddie starts kindergarten on Monday," Tyler said.

"Are you excited?" Leah asked her.

Maddie took a moment to consider her answer, like she seemed to do with most questions. "I think so."

Leah suspected the prospect of not only starting school but also being in a place she didn't know any other children was scary. "I bet you are the smartest kid in the class."

As Leah cut off a bite-size piece of her pork chop, she caught Tyler watching her. He didn't immediately look away as someone might when caught staring. It reawakened the spinning in her middle, which felt as if it had multiplied and spread to all parts of her body, even some she didn't want to think about, not with a child at the table. When he finally broke eye contact, she thought she detected a slight jolt pass through him as if he'd realized too late that she'd caught him staring. Or maybe he'd surprised himself by staring at all. Could he be experiencing the same attraction as well as the same wariness of acknowledging it?

As they finished the meal, Leah couldn't stop

thinking about how to an outside observer they might look like a family having dinner together. She was surprised by how much that image appealed to her. It was enough to make her wonder if she'd cracked her head on the pavement when she'd fallen at the end of the driveway. But though she was still nursing aches from her twin falls, her head wasn't among them.

No, somehow a door to part of her heart had opened to admit this man and his sweet niece. If she were to share what she was feeling with her parents, Conner, even Reina, she suspected they might believe it a result of her ordeal. Even she wondered if these feelings of tenderness and desire to connect were because her heart and soul were looking for something positive, something reassuring, something healing. How could she be sure what she was feeling was real, however improbable that might be, or simply a means to an emotional end?

Maddie slid the bakery bag toward Leah, pulling her away from all the questions blazing a path through her mind.

"Thank you for these," Leah said. "Don't you have a cookie?"

Tyler leaned back in his chair. "This one had her cookie eaten before we even got out of town."

He obviously meant his words as teasing, but Leah saw something pass over Maddie's face that her uncle didn't. She knew that look, had worn it herself countless times in recent weeks. But why would Maddie be scared now? Regardless of the reason, the need to comfort her overrode everything else. She placed her hand atop Maddie's and gently squeezed.

"That's okay. Sometimes you just can't wait to eat

a good cookie." Leah took a bite of her own and didn't have to fake her enjoyment of it. Keri Teague was a talented baker, and everyone in town and probably for miles in all directions knew it.

Leah ate one of her cookies, then told Maddie she was going to save the other one for later. She helped Tyler clear the table, carrying the dishes to the sink. As if it were the most natural thing in the world, as if they were a real family and had shared this task countless times before, they stood side by side, Tyler washing the dishes and Leah rinsing and placing them in the drainer.

Tyler extended the final plate to her, and when she reached for it their fingers grazed each other. It was over in a moment, but the touch rocketed up her arm to explode like fireworks all throughout her body. What was going on? She barely knew Tyler. And after what she'd suffered, how did the intensity of her attraction make any sense? She tried to pretend she hadn't noticed, but she sensed Tyler stiffen beside her and heard the slight hitch in his breath. It wasn't just her having these strange and unexpected reactions, and that scared her more than if she'd been alone in them.

Tyler grabbed a towel and dried his hands. "I think it's someone's bedtime," he said as he turned toward the table.

Leah expected Maddie to beg for more time, that she wasn't tired, but she didn't. Of course, Maddie wasn't like most children. Leah thought back to the look she'd seen on the girl's face earlier and wished she could ask her about it.

"Do you know any bedtime stories, Leah?"

"I could tell you a story." The hope in Tyler's

voice nearly broke Leah's heart, and it was only compounded when she saw the way the light dimmed ever so slightly in Maddie's eyes.

Leah glanced at Tyler and saw that he'd witnessed it, as well. What had changed since she'd seen niece and uncle walking hand in hand earlier? Maybe if she could talk to Maddie alone, she could find out the answer to the perplexing question, help these two grow closer.

"I might know a story or two," she said. "If that's okay with your uncle."

When Tyler nodded, Leah had to resist the urge to go to him, to tell him to just give Maddie time, that his niece would eventually shed her caution. But she shouldn't promise something she couldn't be certain would happen.

Tyler's gaze caught hers for a moment before she ushered Maddie toward the stairs. Leah suspected her willingness to tell bedtime stories might have just as much to do with Tyler as it did Maddie. After that moment at the sink and how her nerves had sizzled when she caught him staring at her, she wasn't sure she should be alone with Tyler. And it wasn't him she didn't trust. It was herself.

Chapter Nine

Leah told Maddie a story she made up as she went, about a little princess who lived in a tower room and whose best friend was a talking baby bear. While Maddie seemed to enjoy the story, Leah could tell something still weighed on her young mind. She captured one of Maddie's hands and pressed it gently between hers.

"Honey, can you tell me what is troubling you?"

Maddie glanced toward the door, almost as if she expected to see a monster come to life there. "I don't want to make Uncle Tyler mad."

Leah's heart froze. Was she wrong about Tyler? Could he be cruel and very good at hiding it?

Keeping her voice low, she asked, "Has he hurt you?"

How quickly Maddie shook her head eased Leah's worry, but something still wasn't right.

"Has he yelled at you? Threatened to punish you?"

"No."

Keeping her voice gentle, Leah asked, "Why do you think he'd be mad at you?"

Maddie shrugged, but unshed tears shone in her pretty blue eyes.

"Does this have something to do with your mom?"

"She got mad and didn't want me anymore."

Leah was not a violent person by nature, and recent events made her loathe violence even more. But in that moment, she thought she might be able to ignore her aversion and do Kendra bodily harm.

"Maddie, honey, did your mother hurt you?"

The child looked as if she wasn't sure she should answer.

"I promise you won't get into trouble if you tell me. You're safe here."

"Mark, that's Mom's boyfriend, told her I cost too much, to give me away."

Anger like she'd never felt in her entire life burst into an inferno inside Leah, but she did her best to hide that from Maddie. The last thing the girl needed was to be scared of another adult.

"He shouldn't have said that. It's not true. And you know what else?"

Maddie shook her head on her pillow.

"Your uncle won't let anything bad happen to you. He loves you."

"He does?" Maddie sounded as if she wasn't sure Leah was telling her the truth. Maybe she was afraid to believe it, afraid she'd be hurt again.

Leah nodded. She heard the creak of the stairs but didn't let on to Maddie that her uncle was right outside. Leah wondered how much he'd heard.

"Are you sure?" Maddie asked, a tentative hope in her voice.

"Positive. I can see it in his eyes. And eyes don't lie."

After Leah said that, she sensed the anxiety inside

Maddie ease. And as Leah told her one more tale of the princess and her pet bear, Maddie fell asleep.

Leah didn't immediately leave the bedroom, which she suspected from the decor had once been Kendra's. Instead, she sat on the side of the bed and watched Maddie fall deeper into sleep. Only when she was certain she wouldn't wake her by moving did she ease Maddie's hand onto the summer quilt under which the girl slept, and quietly left the room.

She was careful with her steps down the stairs, not wanting them to creak any more than stairs in an older house had to. When she reached the lower level, she didn't see Tyler anywhere. Thinking he might have gone outside to check on the horses, she stepped out the front door. She found him pacing the porch, and in the dark he was even more imposing. Fighting her gut reaction to go back inside or make for the bunkhouse, she turned to face him. Even in the dim light coming from inside the house, she was able to see the anger on his face. It told her what she'd suspected.

"You heard everything?"

"How can someone do that to their own child?"

His raised voice made Leah take a step back. She understood his anger, but having it come from someone so much larger than her, a man, unnerved her.

Tyler noticed and stopped his pacing. "I'm sorry. I'm just so…" He wiped his hand down over his face, which reflected an agony she wished she could soothe. "I feel like such a failure. My niece is afraid to even talk to me. I wasn't able to keep my sister from destroying her own life."

Leah couldn't stand the raw pain she heard in his

voice and closed the distance between them. Though she shook as she placed her hand on his arm.

"It's not your fault. Sometimes we can do everything that's possible and bad things still happen."

"But—"

"Stop blaming yourself. It won't change the past and can actually hurt the future." Is that what she'd been doing unconsciously, blaming herself for not being more aware of her surroundings?

She mentally shook her head. No. How could she have possibly known that a man bent on doing her harm had found a way into her home while she was gone?

Stop thinking about that. Now isn't the time.

Tyler met her gaze, and his softened. He placed his hand atop hers where it lay against his upper arm. Her breath caught as she looked up at him. She couldn't see the color of his eyes out here, but she saw it in her mind.

"Thank you," he said.

"For what?" Her words came out a little shaky.

"Taking an interest in Maddie, telling her the stories, reassuring her." He paused, running his thumb across the back of her hand. "For telling her that I love her, because I do. I did from the moment I met her tiny little face in the hospital after she was born. She was only minutes old and crying like crazy, but I didn't think I'd ever seen anything more beautiful."

Something moved in Leah's heart. Tyler Lowe appeared to be the type of man with whom women fell head over heels in love, probably had even though he for some reason remained single. She wasn't sure she wasn't tumbling down that path herself. What wasn't to love? He took in his niece and loved her to pieces, did his best to provide for her, had been kind to Leah in her hour of need, as well. Not to mention he was gorgeous. There was no other word for the way the man looked. She suddenly wished she'd met him before Garton invaded her life, that the attack had never happened.

But then she and Tyler might never have met.

She became intensely aware of how he was looking at her, like he was every bit as attracted as she was. Excitement bubbled up within her, but when he leaned toward her she stepped back from him without conscious thought. It was the damned self-protective instinct overriding the very real desire to know what it would feel like to have Tyler kiss her. Would she ever get past that dark nugget of fear within herself that made her worry that Tyler might hurt her? Had Garton irreparably scarred her? Destroyed her ability to trust?

"It's getting late. I better grab my laundry and turn in. I've got some errands to run tomorrow."

Tyler nodded and took his own step back. "I should have your new water heater installed by the time you get home."

"Thank you. And thank you for dinner, and for letting me use the shower and the laundry room."

Tyler smiled, making her wish she hadn't broken contact with him.

"It sounds like we're having a contest to see who can thank the other the most," he said.

She laughed a little. "Then I'll just say good-night. And… I know it's hard, but give Maddie time. She considers things carefully, especially for someone her age. I have faith she will see the truth of what I told her about you."

"I hope you're right."

As Leah hurried up the drive a few minutes later, laundry basket in hand and trying to ignore the darkness pressing in on her, stealing her breath, she hoped she was right, too. That she hadn't given Tyler false hope.

DESPITE WHAT LEAH had said, Tyler didn't see any difference in how Maddie acted around him. She replied when he asked her questions, but beyond that she spent her time playing outside, watching cartoons or coloring. A few times he'd notice her forehead furrowed as if she were thinking hard. It reminded him of something else Leah had said the night before, that Maddie took her time to think things through and that he had to have faith that his niece would come around.

Thinking of Leah also brought back the memory of how small and soft her hand had felt beneath his, how he would have kissed her had she not stepped away. Again, he'd sensed a layer of fear in her, increasing his belief that someone had hurt her.

He let out a long breath. Why did people have to hurt each other? It made no sense.

He'd spent the morning getting her new water heater installed, but Leah had already been gone by the time he returned from town with it. Already the bunkhouse felt wrong when she wasn't there.

Now, as he drove out to the Brody ranch to tend to a couple of horses Owen Brody was training for rodeo stock, his thoughts shifted back to Maddie. He glanced over toward her, saw she was hugging her ever-present stuffed puppy. Out of the blue, he remembered a little green stuffed frog that Kendra had carried around when she'd been little more than Maddie's age. He smiled when he remembered her telling their mother that one day she would kiss the frog and he'd be a prince.

Had his sister been kissing frogs ever since in hopes of finding her prince? Tears threatened to blur his vision at how lost his sister was. Sometimes he felt just as lost.

He shoved heavy thoughts away as he pulled into the Brody ranch and waved at Owen and his wife, Linnea.

"Hello," Linnea said as Tyler helped Maddie out of the truck. "This must be your niece."

Tyler made the introductions.

"Maddie, I just made a batch of cookies. Would you help me out by testing one to see if it's good or not?" Linnea smiled as she met Tyler's gaze.

Maddie looked up at him, as well. "Can I?"

"Sure."

Tyler noticed the way Owen watched his wife lead Maddie toward the house, a smile of contentment on his face. "Seems married life is agreeing with you."

"It is indeed. You should try it yourself."

An image of Leah in his arms, looking up at him with love and admiration, shook Tyler. He forced his mind away from that thought and back to Owen.

"Owen Brody, giving out relationship advice. How the world has changed."

"Don't knock it till you try it." Owen slapped him on the back as he directed Tyler toward the barn.

Tyler pulled out his tools as Owen positioned the horse so Tyler could trim its hooves.

"Heard you rented out your bunkhouse to Conner's cousin."

"Yep. Building was just sitting there. Figured it might as well be earning me some money."

"Leah's a pretty woman. Maybe you won't have to look far for love."

Tyler looked at Owen. "Has Verona Charles infected everyone in town with some matchmaking virus?"

Owen laughed. "Just putting the idea out there."

Tyler didn't need help with that. It seemed he'd been thinking about Leah and how pretty she was since he'd met her. But he didn't need Owen to know that. Or anyone else for that matter.

"Why are you so interested? Did she turn you down too before you got blissfully married?"

"Too?" Owen's eyebrow rose as if he'd caught Tyler in a slipup.

"Yeah. Greg said he asked her out once and she declined."

Owen snorted. "I would have given good money to see the look on his face. But how did you and Greg get on that topic?"

"For some reason, everyone seems to be interested in my love life all of a sudden."

Owen shrugged. "Small town."

"Where gossip is the main form of entertainment." Which was exactly why he didn't need to get involved with Leah. What if they got together and it impacted Maddie in a negative way? He got the impression she hadn't seen any positive instances of people dating.

Plus, what if things didn't work out between him and Leah? How awkward would that be when she came to pay the rent?

Not to mention Leah might not even be interested. He thought he'd seen something in her eyes the night before, felt a shiver go through her body, but there was also his increasing belief that she'd been hurt somehow, that she was more cautious than most women. If so, he needed to be as careful with her as he was Maddie, even more so.

Owen went off to meet with someone interested in buying a horse, leaving Tyler to his work and his thoughts. When he finally finished with the horses, he didn't immediately leave the barn. Instead, he sank onto a wooden bench and leaned back against one of the stalls. He hadn't been sleeping well, all his worries refusing to quiet enough to rest. It felt good to just be for a moment. He had no more work scheduled for today and Maddie was being looked after. He closed his eyes and listened to the shifting and breathing of the horses, smelled fresh hay, felt a gentle breeze drifting through the barn.

The sound of a child's giggling brought him away from the verge of sleep. It took a couple of seconds to realize it was Maddie giggling. He had to see what miracle had brought out that reaction in his niece.

Tyler rose to his feet and walked to the barn's entrance. There on the porch sat Maddie petting the Brodys' two old bassett hounds. One of them licked Maddie's face, making her giggles ring out across the ranch again. It was wonderful to see her happy, and the reason why gave him an idea.

After they returned home and Maddie had gone up

to her room, Tyler spotted Leah out by the line of trees taking photos. He wondered what his reception would be considering how quickly she'd made her departure the night before, but he found himself walking up the drive anyway.

When she noticed him, she stood.

"Taking up nature photography?" he asked as he motioned toward the wildflowers.

"Was just taking a break from work and decided to snap some shots. They're very pretty."

Not as pretty as Leah. But he didn't say that out loud.

She turned to face him. "How are things with Maddie today?"

"About the same, maybe a little better. That's why I'm here. I have a favor to ask."

"Sure, I'll help if I can."

He told her about Maddie's reaction to the dogs at the Brody ranch. "I want to get her a puppy. Would you go to the shelter with me when she's in school tomorrow?"

Leah smiled. "That's a great idea. I'd love to help."

Tyler breathed a little easier that the uneasiness he'd seen in her eyes the night before had disappeared with the light of day. And though it wasn't a date, he was already looking forward to spending time alone with her.

LEAH PACED HER living area, ridiculously nervous about going to the animal shelter with Tyler. And this time it wasn't because she was scared he might hurt her. It was the being alone with him after the way he'd looked at her the night on the porch, the way his hand had felt atop hers—gentle with a layer of roughness that came from good, honest work.

She realized in that moment that even Tyler's career showed he was a person who cared for others, animals included. Even his idea of getting Maddie a puppy showed he knew how important connections were, how a pet could sometimes soothe hurts that words couldn't.

Already, she considered Tyler a friend. The fact it had happened so quickly surprised her since it came so soon after her attack. That she'd allowed him to touch her, more than once, spoke to something else entirely. Something she wasn't sure she was ready to explore.

But how could she refuse him when he was trying so hard to connect with his niece, to help Maddie trust him?

At least Leah wouldn't be riding with him in the close confines of his truck. She'd heard him leave a few minutes earlier to take Maddie to her first day of school. Leah had told him the previous evening that it didn't make sense for him to return to the ranch to pick her up, so she was to meet him at the shelter.

If she got up the nerve to walk out her front door.

Leah stopped pacing. "Don't overthink it. You're going to pick out a puppy, for heaven's sake."

She grabbed her purse and a few boxes filled with jewelry orders she needed to drop off at the post office, and headed out the door.

By the time she reached the animal shelter, Tyler was already there, sitting on the open tailgate of his truck. A man shouldn't look so delicious without even making any effort. As she hesitated getting out of her car, she wondered what Tyler Lowe was hiding under that short-sleeved, button-up shirt. If it was anything like the arms and hands she could see, it might cause her to have heart palpitations. Were those kinds of thoughts a sign she was beginning to get past what had happened to her or just the power of Tyler's attractiveness?

Puppies, puppies, puppies. Think about puppies.

"Thought maybe you'd changed your mind," Tyler said when she finally stepped out of the car.

"Long line at the post office." And a long line of competing thoughts in her head.

"Always is on Monday."

He held the door to the building open for her, adding evidence to the case that he was a good guy.

They were met by a pixieish young woman at the front desk. "How can I help you?"

"I'd like to adopt a puppy for my niece."

Pixie girl, whose name turned out to be Clary, launched into several questions: How old was his niece? Did he live in town or in the country? Were there other pets in the home?

When she finally finished, Tyler said, "I feel like I've just been interviewed for a position with the CIA."

Clary laughed. "It is a lot, but we use the information to make sure the animals are going to a safe environment and we pair you with the best possible match. Could your niece come in to interact with the puppies?"

"It's a surprise."

Clary nodded. "Okay. If you'll follow me."

Again Tyler let Leah precede him, holding open the door that led back to the kennels. She wasn't the type of woman who needed men to do everything for her, but a girl could get used to a little chivalry doled out by a handsome cowboy.

"Take a walk through and see if any of these little guys and girls look promising," Clary said. "You can interact with however many you want to until you find the right one for your niece."

As if they smelled freedom and a new life, the wide variety of puppies barked and wagged their tails as they stood at the front of their cages.

"There are so many," Leah said as they slowly walked down the line. "Makes me want to take all of them."

"You might have a new job as puppy wrangler then," Tyler said.

"There are worse jobs."

"Until you have to clean up all the puppy poop."

"You make an excellent point. Although it is a ranch with lots of fields. And the cows already fertilize the place."

"And feed themselves for the most part."

"Oh, you and your facts."

Tyler laughed then stuck his finger inside the cage with an adorable little beagle. The puppy licked his finger with a lot of enthusiasm.

Clary opened the cage and placed the puppy on the floor. Leah watched as Tyler got down on one knee and played with the little guy. Something about that pose, down on one knee, caused her breath to catch.

Needing to look at anything but an impossibly handsome man playing with an impossibly cute puppy, she walked down another row of cages. When she came to the last one, she noticed the brown puppy inside didn't come to the front to greet her like the others. Instead, he was curled in on himself in the back corner, a thick bandage wrapped around one of his hind legs. She noticed the tag on the outside of the cage said he was a mixed breed and his name was Fēlix.

Carly stepped up beside her. "This is one of the ones that break your heart."

"What happened to him?" Leah carefully placed her fingers around the wire mesh of the cage and wiggled them slowly.

"He was found in a ditch, shivering, with a broken leg."

"Someone hit him?"

"Worse. Someone threw him out the window of a truck then sped off. There was a witness, but he wasn't close enough to get a license plate."

Leah's heart broke right there.

A ding indicated someone else had come into the front office of the shelter, requiring Clary's attention.

Leah moved closer to the cage and looked into Felix's eyes. He might be a puppy, but she felt an immediate bond with him. They'd both been brutalized and now harbored fear and distrust because of it.

"Hey, sweetie," she said. "Aren't you a handsome fella?"

To her surprise, Felix slowly started to uncurl himself, paused then got to his feet and hobbled cautiously to the front of the cage. She let Felix make the first contact, though it took him several tries. She nearly cried at how it was obvious he wanted to believe she was trustworthy but was scarred from his experience, and not just physically. It was as if she were looking at a canine version of herself.

And she knew that even if she had to move again, she wasn't leaving this building without this poor, broken puppy. He would know that despite the cruelty he'd experienced, there was at least one person in the world who loved him. That he was worthy of love and a life that was as filled with happiness as it could be.

Leah slowly turned her head to look at Tyler, and wondered if she could have the same thing, too.

Chapter Ten

Tyler was glad Leah had adopted a puppy, as well. One look at the little guy in her arms, at the look of pure love and devotion on her face, and he'd known it was meant to be. That he'd immediately wondered what it would be like if she wore that look for him… Well, she didn't need to know that.

But if she'd been through something that hurt her, maybe little Felix was just what she needed.

He watched as she put a puppy bed in her cart.

"I guess the store hit the jackpot with us today," he said as he reached up above her and grabbed a chew toy she'd been trying to reach while standing on her tiptoes.

"Yeah." She accepted the toy. "Thanks. Sucks being short sometimes."

"Bet you don't have to worry about knocking your head as often as I do."

"True."

"I'm glad you're getting Felix," he said as he pushed his cart along behind hers.

She glanced over her shoulder. "Really?"

"Yeah. The ones who've been through the wringer often get overlooked."

Leah stared at him for a moment, as if she were trying to figure out if he meant more than he said.

Trying too hard, pal. Abort!

He pushed his cart to the other side of the aisle and grabbed a bag of puppy food. "Yeah, and once Felix heals, he and Baxter can play together."

Did that sound too connected? Too long-term? He just needed to shut up before he dug his hole any deeper.

"Well, hello there."

Oh, hell. As if he needed more fuel for the fire.

"Hey, Verona," he said. "How are you today?"

"Great. How about you?" Verona patted him on the arm, then didn't give him time to answer before turning toward Leah. "Your new living arrangements must be working out if you two are shopping together already."

Leah looked like a startled deer caught in head-lights.

"I got my niece a puppy today, and Leah was kind enough to help me pick out one."

"That was nice of you," she said to Leah. But then she glanced between the two carts. "How big is this puppy that it needs two beds?"

"While we were there, I spotted another puppy that had been abused. I just couldn't leave without giving him a home," Leah said.

"What a kind heart you have, dear." Verona looked back at Tyler for a moment before going on. "You'll make someone a wonderful wife someday. Don't you think so, Tyler?"

Elissa Kayne, Verona's niece, swooped in to the awkward scene, hooking her arm around her aunt's and guiding her on down the aisle. "Sorry, guys," she called back over her shoulder. "She's normally better behaved."

Tyler couldn't help it. He snorted out a laugh.

"I see Verona's upped her game," Leah said.

"So you're aware of her reputation."

"Oh yeah. Conner is perfecting the art of avoiding her."

"Smart man."

When Leah glanced at him, he couldn't read the expression on her face. He got the oddest impression that it was at least partly disappointment. He was still trying to figure it out when they paid for their purchases and left the store.

"You want to grab some lunch?" he asked, surprising himself. He shouldn't be asking Leah to be seen with him in yet another public spot if he wanted to get Verona off their case, but he couldn't seem to help it. The more time he spent with Leah, the more he liked her. She was the type of woman who reassured little girls and adopted injured puppies. And as if that weren't enough, she was the most beautiful woman he'd ever seen. How many times had he thought about running his fingers through her hair, kissing her pink lips, pulling her close and protecting her from whatever terror had truly been chasing her that night she'd fallen outside the barn?

"You're not afraid of giving Verona more ammunition?"

"Verona will believe what she wants to, no matter what we do or say. Plus, we can always tell her that someone who really needs her skills as a matchmaker is Conner."

Leah laughed so suddenly, she snorted. She covered her mouth, obviously embarrassed.

Tyler just smiled and opened the door to his truck. "Meet you at the Primrose."

He began second-guessing his decision to ask her to lunch almost from the moment they sat down at a table in the café. It was as if the heads of all the locals swiveled their way, like lions sensing fresh meat. What if Leah didn't want people thinking they were a couple or on their way to being one? Maybe she had good reasons for not wanting a relationship, with anyone. He had to act casual despite the fact that being with her made him want to grin like a fool.

"So, how did things go when you dropped off Maddie at school this morning?"

"She was quiet, as usual. She looked so tiny walking down the hall to her classroom. Her backpack was half as big as she was."

"I remember that feeling. By the time I got to high school, I think my books weighed almost what I did."

"I can't imagine."

Leah smiled. "Of course not. You're as tall as a tree."

They talked about her family and how her best friend was currently pregnant but wanted to come visit her as soon as she could after giving birth.

An image of Leah rounded with a child popped into his head, causing him to choke on an onion ring.

"You okay?" Leah asked.

Still coughing, he nodded. After he managed to down some water, he brought the choking under control. He motioned to his throat. "Went the wrong way."

The same as his thoughts.

LEAH DIDN'T HAVE the heart to put Felix back in a cage as she drove home. So the little guy was lying on her lap. He'd been shaking so much that she began driving with one hand and rubbing his back with the other. The shaking had slowly stopped, but she kept her hand on his back, reassuring him that he was safe.

With Felix calmed, her thoughts drifted to how much time she'd spent with Tyler today, how easy it had been between them. Even when Verona had put them in a potentially awkward position. It made Leah wonder things that she probably shouldn't.

But honestly, how was she supposed to prevent herself from wondering what it would be like to be with Tyler? He was handsome, kind, funny when he wanted to be, caring and had even seemed genuinely interested in how she'd started her jewelry business while in college and how she'd built it. Yes, his size still intimidated her some, but oddly she found it reassuring, as well.

By the time she got home, unloaded everything and got Felix settled, it was time to head down to the house. She'd told Tyler that she would check on Baxter and keep the puppy quiet until Tyler was ready to reveal him to Maddie. By the way Baxter barked when she stepped into the house, she had her work cut out for her.

"Come here, little guy," she said as she picked up Baxter and cuddled him against her. She laughed when he licked her cheek.

With the puppy in her arms, she wandered over to the fireplace on the opposite side of the living room to examine the framed photos along the mantel. It struck her that none of them seemed recent. The older couple had to be Tyler's parents, and then there were photos of Tyler and a girl who was most likely Kendra at various ages.

She lifted a finger and ran it across Tyler's face in what appeared to be the most recent shot of him and Kendra. While he was smiling, she saw the beginning of the heartache in his eyes caused by his sister's addiction. If she looked closely, she could see the change in Kendra in the picture, too. Even at such a young age, she was already on the road that had led her to abandoning her daughter.

The sound of Tyler's truck sent her hurrying for the laundry room. She closed the door most of the way, leaving a crack so she could hear her cue to let Baxter loose.

Baxter wiggled, trying to get out of her arms.

"Shh," she said close to his floppy little ear.

The front door opened, and Leah listened to the sound of Tyler's boots against the wooden floor in the living room.

"I'm glad you had a good first day of school," Tyler said. "Before you go upstairs, I have a surprise for you."

Leah peeked through the door in time to see Maddie turn toward her uncle and look up at him. "A surprise?"

When Tyler whistled, Leah opened the door and let Baxter go. His toenails clicked against the floor and slid as he tried to find purchase. As if he knew his intended target, he raced straight for Maddie.

"A puppy!" Maddie crouched and Baxter ran right into her, knocking her over and proceeding to lick her face.

Maddie's giggling was one of the happiest sounds Leah had ever heard.

"Is he really mine?" Maddie asked, so much tentative hope in her voice.

"He is. His name is Baxter."

"Baxter." Maddie said his name with awe and hugged his wiggly little body close.

When Baxter broke free to run around the room as if chasing invisible rabbits, Maddie got to her feet and looked at her uncle for a long moment. Then, seeming to make a decision, she ran straight toward him and hugged his jeans-clad legs.

"Thank you, Uncle Tyler. I've always wanted a puppy."

Leah pushed away a burst of anger that this was something else Kendra had denied her child. For this moment, she wanted to focus on the incredible scene in front of her.

Tyler looked so stunned that he didn't immediately move, but then he bent over and picked Maddie up in his arms.

"You're welcome, sweetheart."

When Maddie leaned forward and kissed him on the cheek, he pulled her close for a hug that was a long time coming. As he looked toward Leah, she thought she saw tears in his eyes. Not wanting to distract either of them from this huge breakthrough in their relationship, Leah gave Tyler a smile then slipped out the exterior door on the other side of the laundry room.

TYLER LEANED OVER and turned off Maddie's bedside lamp. His niece was finally asleep after three bedtime stories. He'd not wanted the evening to end, afraid something would drag her back to the silent child she'd mostly been since her arrival. But when her eyes could no longer stay open, he had reluctantly told her that she had to go to sleep so she wouldn't fall asleep in school tomorrow.

Baxter stirred in his bed right next to Maddie's. Tyler leaned down and rubbed the puppy's head.

"Time for you to sleep, too, little guy." Baxter gave Tyler's hand a halfhearted lick that said the puppy was just as tired as his new best friend.

Tyler paused at the door as he left the room, marveling at what a difference a day could make. After gifting her with a puppy, Maddie had said more at dinner, telling him all about her day at school and her new friend Olivia, than she'd said during all the time since Kendra had left her with him.

He eased down the stairs but then didn't know what to do with himself. He had financial records to update, but that held about as much appeal as being bucked off a horse. Instead, he walked out onto the porch and took a breath of fresh evening air. As was typical now, his gaze drifted to the bunkhouse.

Leah had left before he'd had an opportunity to thank her again for all her help. No time like the present.

When he knocked on her door, at first he didn't think she would answer. Could she be asleep already? The slight creak of what he thought might be a floorboard met his ear right before he saw Leah peek out the window. A moment later, she opened the door.

"Hey, is something wrong?"

He shook his head. "No. I just wanted to thank you for your help earlier."

"No need. Things still going well?"

"Yes. Maddie and Baxter are both asleep, worn out from playing with each other."

Leah smiled, filling his heart with a lightness that pulled at him like gravity.

"I'm glad to hear it. When Maddie ran into your arms, I darn near cried right on the spot."

"You're not the only one. And then…" He paused and swallowed against the catch in his throat. "She asked me to tell her bedtime stories. I haven't been able to do that since she was really little."

It hit him that none of the other family members who'd been a part of his life then were around any longer. His parents, gone. Kendra…he worried every day that he'd get a call from some unknown person, informing him as her next of kin that she was gone, as well. The knot in his throat grew larger, and he spun away from Leah and put a little more distance between them. The enormity of the fact that the person who'd done the most for him lately was someone he'd known less than a month hit him square in his middle, stealing his breath. Staring out into the darkness, he sank onto the edge of the porch.

Behind him, Leah stepped out of the bunkhouse and shut the door. She came to sit beside him.

"Want to talk about it?" she asked.

"I don't know what's wrong with me. I should be happy as a clam right now."

"Sometimes things just build up over time, especially ones we can't control. I know guys are all macho and stuff, don't want to show their feelings, and I respect that to a certain extent. But it's just common sense that keeping everything bottled up isn't the best way to deal with problems. It's like an infection, needs air to heal."

He glanced over at her, how she'd pulled back her hair in a ponytail. "You sure you weren't a counselor in a previous life?"

"That would be ironic."

"How so?"

She waved away his question. "Tell me about Kendra when she was a kid. I saw some pictures on your mantel earlier of you two when you were younger. You looked happy."

He sighed. He tried not to think too much of those days now. They just made him sad and feel like more of a failure.

"We were. Kendra was actually a lot like Maddie when she was little, at least how Maddie was when she was a toddler. She was curious, ran all over this ranch, but she was also fearless, willing to try anything. Dad encouraged that, but Mom was always afraid one day Kendra would go too far. And she did."

"How old was she when she started using?"

"Seventeen, I think. She might have experimented sooner. But that's when she acquired her first in a string of loser boyfriends. Suddenly she went from a pretty good kid to acting out, smarting off to my parents, telling me to stop trying to tell her what to do. She ran away once, but I managed to track her down and bring her home. She still hasn't forgiven me for that. At least not on the days she can even remember her own name."

"I'm so sorry, Tyler. I know it's hard. Watching Reina's family deal with her brother's abuse was heartbreaking." She paused and clasped her hands together between her knees. "Do you think there's any hope of her agreeing to rehab?"

"About as much as my cows turning into unicorns."

"I take it your parents have passed?"

He nodded. "When Maddie was about one. Dad had a stroke, and Mom died a couple of months later. Doctors said it was probably her heart. I agreed, though my diagnosis was a broken heart. Both because of losing Dad and how Kendra would disappear for months at a time, leaving us all wondering if we'd ever see her or Maddie again. I wish I'd done more to try to get through to Kendra, or at least protect Maddie."

He hung his head, fighting the need to cry and yell at the top of his lungs at the same time.

"You're too hard on yourself," Leah said.

"You don't know that."

"I do."

He looked up at her and saw the absolute certainty in her expression.

"Everything I've seen of you since we met tells me you're someone who cares for others, that you want to make things right. A guy like that isn't one who wouldn't have done everything in his power to help his sister and niece."

She couldn't possibly know how much those words meant to him. Her belief in him gave him the courage to voice something he'd been thinking about for several days, honestly since Kendra had left Maddie with him.

"I'm not letting Kendra take Maddie back, not unless she's clean and gets her life on track. And stays away from all pitiful excuses for men. I'll do whatever I have to." Even if it put him on the wrong side of the law. If he lost the ranch, everything he'd worked for, he'd do it to protect Maddie.

"Good."

"Good? You realize courts almost always side with the mother."

"I can't see any judge leaving a five-year-old with an addict with Kendra's history, not when there is a solid, loving, safe alternative with another family member."

Tyler let Leah's words soak into him like a balm. They were exactly what he needed to hear without realizing it.

"I'm glad you moved here," he said.

"You are?" Her eyes widened, as if she could sense the direction his thoughts had turned.

He moved slowly as he lifted his hand, aware of how skittish she often was around him. When he placed his palm against her cheek, he felt her stiffen and a shudder race through her body. "I won't hurt you, Leah."

He leaned toward her, expecting her to bolt at any moment. When she didn't, he lowered his lips to hers.

LEAH'S HEART BEAT so fast that she felt it throughout her entire body. One part of her mind was yelling, "Danger! Danger! Danger!" But another part wanted to sink in to Tyler's kiss, to fully enjoy this moment that she'd thought about so many times in recent days. She wanted to trust his words, that he wouldn't hurt her. He'd given her no reason not to.

Her desire overrode her caution and she responded to the kiss. Flames licked her skin as she felt Tyler's body heat move closer. This was nice, really nice. His woodsy male scent tickled her nose, and her hands somehow found his broad shoulders. A flutter of panic threatened to ruin the moment, but she pushed it away. At least until she felt his hand on the side of her neck. His big, powerful hand.

Leah broke the kiss and leaped to her feet in the same motion.

Tyler started to stand as well but seemed to catch himself, realizing it was a bad idea. "Did I hurt you?"

Leah desperately tried to rein in her panic because there was no threat. It was some prehistoric part of her brain sending flight signals that weren't needed. Still, she couldn't seem to calm her racing heart.

"No, I'm fine. Just…surprised, maybe."

Surprised she'd been able to respond so quickly to him, of how much a part of her wished she hadn't broken the kiss and was in his arms.

"I'm sorry if I did something you didn't want."

She shook her head. "It's not you, it's me. I know that's a cliché, but it's the truth." She forced herself to breathe more slowly. "I'm sorry. I just…can't."

Tyler nodded. She saw disappointment in his eyes but also acceptance. It made her want to take it back, to continue what they'd started. But she could still feel his hand running over the part of her neck Garton had gripped as he'd held her down. The all-consuming fear she'd felt that night, convinced he was going to crush her throat when he was done with her, threatened to swamp her like a rogue wave. She needed to get inside, to put up literal walls between her and the outside world.

She watched as Tyler walked away from the porch toward the driveway.

"I'll wait until you're inside."

She watched him for a moment, hating how her fear was winning over the part of her that wanted to go to him, to give him the support and tenderness he needed in his life. But she was just the wrong woman at the wrong time.

Her heart heavy, she stepped up onto the porch and crossed to the door. She paused after she opened the door and looked back at him, dimly illuminated by the light spilling from her living room.

"Good night, Tyler."

"Good night, Leah."

A man of his word, he waited until she was inside with the door locked before he headed down the driveway. As she listened to the sound of his boots on the gravel, tears spilled over onto her cheeks as she sank to the floor.

As if it was his turn to comfort her, Felix hobbled over to her, holding up his bandaged leg, and curled next to her side. Leah cried even harder at the thought that Felix was the only man she'd ever trust again.

Chapter Eleven

Leah timed her departure from the ranch the next morning so that she didn't run into Tyler. She wasn't upset with him, but she also didn't want to get into the why behind her actions the night before. The same reasons that had her tripping and falling outside the barn the night he'd helped her. An unreasonable fear that now that she'd been attacked once, it might happen again.

In the light of day, it made even less sense to think that Tyler would hurt her. He'd had plenty of opportunities but had been nothing but a gentleman. Shouldn't she be thankful to have found such a man, one who had at least some interest in her?

She sighed, so very tired of having arguments with herself. One minute a voice in her head would say she should learn to live again and see where things with Tyler might go. But then another voice would warn that if things didn't work out, he could pose a danger and it was better to be safe than sorry. Honestly, she felt like she was going mad.

Better to focus on something, anything, other than Tyler and her conflicting feelings toward him. She grabbed the boxes of completed jewelry and headed out to her car. Once inside the car, she chose some up-beat Celtic pub rock to play, hoping to lift her mood and banish thoughts that she might have ruined the new friendship she had with Tyler.

No, stop thinking about Tyler.

Yeah, easier said than done. Ugh.

She drove into Blue Falls and found a parking spot on Main Street a few doors down from her destination, India Parrish's Yesterwear Boutique.

India looked up from where she was doing paperwork at a carved table in the back corner of the entry area and smiled.

"Hey, Leah. It's good to see you." She got to her feet and came toward Leah, pointing at the boxes in Leah's hands. "Tell me that's what I think it is."

In response, Leah opened the top box, revealing a blue-and-green beaded necklace, the multiple strands of which entwined like vines. "I'm sorry it took so long to get a new selection for you to choose from."

India waved her hand. "I'll take it all."

"All of it?"

"Yes, I already have a list of customers I'm supposed to call as soon as your new items arrive."

"Really?"

"Don't sound so surprised. Your stuff is beautiful. And it's perfect for the customers who shop someplace like this."

Leah glanced into the main showroom, at the collections of clothing and accessories displayed by the era that inspired them. "I tried to keep in mind different time periods when making some of these, but some are just general and can go with anything."

"Sounds perfect." India took the boxes out of Leah's

hands and placed them atop the glass display case next to the cash register. "Come on, have a pastry and coffee with me."

"I don't want to interrupt your work."

"Please interrupt my work. The financials are making my eyes cross. Plus, I have fresh pastries from the bakery."

"Tempting me with Keri's baking. How am I supposed to say no to that?"

"You're not." India hooked her arm through Leah's and guided her toward the table.

As Leah took a seat, India poured her a cup of coffee and opened the white bakery box so Leah could have her pick.

"So, how are you liking your new place? I hear you got a puppy."

Leah chose a cinnamon muffin and placed it on a napkin. "Well, I'm going to have to get used to how fast word travels here."

"Elissa told me she saw you and Tyler at the store buying puppy supplies, and that Verona went full-on matchmaker on you."

Leah gripped her cup harder as her thoughts went back to the kiss she and Tyler had shared and the way she'd reacted first one way and then the opposite. She'd probably given him mental whiplash.

"Is something wrong?"

Leah met her friend's gaze and saw genuine concern there. "No, I'm fine."

"Are you sure?"

Leah knew she didn't sound convincing, not even to herself. She simply couldn't muster the energy to make the appropriate effort. "It's just…some parts of living here are not what I expected."

India tilted her head a bit. "This have to do with Tyler?"

"What makes you say that?"

"Well, one, your mood changed as soon as I mentioned Verona's matchmaking efforts. And I'm also well acquainted with the turmoil that comes from liking someone and wondering if it's wise."

"Glad to know I'm so transparent." She picked at the top of her muffin, no longer truly interested in eating it.

"Let me just tell you this. I've known Tyler a long time, and he's one of the nicest guys you'll ever meet."

"I know."

"But you're not interested?" India sounded confused, and Leah couldn't blame her.

"It's not that simple." Leah stopped fiddling with the muffin, surprised by the sudden need to unburden herself, to talk to someone who wasn't Reina, a cop or related to her. "I do like Tyler. He's a good person. We… He kissed me last night."

"But that's not a good thing?"

"It was, at first. But then it changed." She waved off how that sounded, like Tyler might have done something bad. "It was me." She paused, remembering how she didn't want to be seen as a victim. But wasn't that how she still thought of herself? "I moved here because I wanted to get away from Houston, from what happened to me there."

She shared the story of her coming home after having dinner with her parents and being attacked in her apartment. How she'd had to fight with every ounce of strength she had to break free, to avoid more than the scratches and bruises Garton had left her with. That and a fear that threatened to cripple her.

"But he didn't…?"

Leah shook her head. "No, but I can still feel his hands on my skin. It crawls just thinking about it."

"So when Tyler touched you, it all came back."

"Yeah."

India reached across the table and clasped Leah's hands. "I'm so sorry. I know you'll have to heal at your own pace, but when you're ready, Tyler is a good choice. I'd stake my life on him not hurting you in any way."

"You know what's so confusing? A part of me would, too. Just seeing him with Maddie is enough to tell me that."

"But you're not dealing with rational thought when someone violates your sense of safety that way."

"It feels like I'm insane, with competing voices in my head."

"Don't be so hard on yourself," India said, echoing what Leah had told Tyler. "It doesn't seem like it, but it'll get better. Maybe the key is to just continue to try to move forward, a little bit at a time."

That might not be possible with Tyler, though. She may have already destroyed that chance. Guys likely didn't want to be with women who acted as if their kisses were from a monster.

A couple of women entered the boutique then, requiring India's attention.

"Give me a few minutes, okay?" India said.

"I actually need to go. More errands to run." The

truth was she needed time alone to think, to try to get the voices in her head down to one.

"Okay. Come back anytime you want to talk." India gave her a hug before stepping into the next room to help her customers.

Once she was seated back in her car, Leah wasn't sure where to go. She couldn't leave Felix alone for long, but she wasn't ready to go back to the ranch yet. What if Tyler was there? What in the world was she going to say when she saw him? Maybe he'd avoid her altogether and she wouldn't have to find out.

That thought made her heart ache. India was right. Tyler was a good guy, probably one of the nicest ones she'd ever meet. One who posed little threat, her rational side knew. But how did she convince her fearful brain of that fact? How did she convince him that she was truly sorry?

She wasn't sure how long she sat in her car, but she felt like she couldn't leave until she came to some sort of decision. Oddly, the sight of Verona Charles stepping into a shop down the street helped her make it. She was done with letting Jason Garton ruin her life. Yes, there was still fear within her and might always be to some extent. But she wanted to start shoving some of that fear aside to make room for more trust, for more happiness.

And maybe if she was very lucky, part of that happiness would come in the form of Tyler Lowe.

TYLER FINISHED SHOEING a horse at the Teague guest ranch and headed back toward town. As much as he loved Maddie, he was glad to be back to work on his own. He didn't have to worry about her being bored or getting hurt, and she was at school learning and making friends. That was what she needed, more positive connections to help her believe that she wasn't going to be uprooted again. He knew he needed to consult an attorney about getting custody of her, but he was trying to make sure he had all his ducks in a row, could put forth the best possible case for becoming her official guardian.

Plus he needed to be less distracted. And try as he might, he couldn't stop thinking about Leah and her reaction to the kiss. Rather, her reactions. Plural. When she'd responded by kissing him back, desire had shot through him like a rocket through his veins. He no longer had to wonder if he was only imagining the looks of interest on her face.

But then she'd jumped away from him as if he'd bitten her. The look in her eyes, as though she was an animal cornered by another ten times its size, had punched him in the gut like a pro boxer. He might not be the root of her fear, but he'd scared her nonetheless.

Common sense said he should leave her be, to let her lead the way in any interactions. But he didn't want her to be scared of him all the time if she continued to live within sight of his home. And, if he were being truthful, he hoped they could get past whatever haunted her because he'd enjoyed that kiss more than he had anything in a long time.

But the big question was how.

As if the universe was taking pity on him, he spotted Conner walking from the sheriff's department office to his patrol car. Not having a clue how he was going to broach the topic of Leah, Tyler whipped into the parking spot next to Conner's.

After shoving the truck into Park, he hesitated a moment before turning off the engine, considering pulling right back out on the road. But then he thought about that look in Leah's eyes again and had to at least try to help her. Seemed he'd gone from bachelor farrier and rancher minding his own business to a bleeding-heart saver of lost souls without any warning.

When he got out of his truck, Conner was leaning against the side of his car.

"Hey, man. Heard you and my cousin are the new owners of a couple of puppies."

"Yep. Maddie is already imagining the two pups being best friends. She talked about it all the way to school this morning." And he hadn't minded one bit. After so many weeks of virtual silence, she had a lot of catching up to do. Hearing her happy and excited about new things in her life lifted his heart like it was tied to a hot air balloon. But he still felt as if he had to hold his breath, that something might make her retreat into her shell.

"Glad to hear she's settling in. And thanks again for renting the place to Leah so quickly."

"No problem."

Silence fell between them, and again Tyler thought about leaving without saying anything about Leah. But then how would he explain why he'd stopped in the first place?

"Something I can help you with?" Conner asked.

"This is awkward, but I'm just going to say it. Has someone hurt Leah?"

Conner's eyes narrowed, and Tyler didn't miss how the man's hands went to his hips, his right near his holstered sidearm. It was probably an unconscious gesture, but all the same it made Tyler squirm.

"Why do you ask that?" Conner was sounding more like a protective big brother than a cousin. But maybe he saw himself in that role since Leah didn't have any brothers, any siblings at all.

"She seems skittish." Before Conner could assume the worst, Tyler further explained. "Like the night she ran off the road. When she came running onto the ranch, it was as if the hounds of hell were chasing her. She was terrified."

"She'd just had a scare. And she's used to living in the city. All the darkness out in the country probably freaked her out."

"It's more than that."

Conner's expression shifted, and Tyler imagined it was the face he used when he interrogated people. "You seem certain of that. Is something going on I need to know about?"

Exactly the question Tyler wanted to ask, but it seemed possessive coming from his direction, especially when he and Leah hadn't known each other that long. But something inside him said that right now, honesty was the best policy.

"I like Leah. A lot. And I don't want to do anything to hurt her, particularly if she's already been hurt."

The tension in Conner's body visibly eased. "It's not my story to tell."

"That tells me I'm right, though."

Conner stared at him for a moment. Tyler could almost hear the decision-making process happening in his head. What to say. How much to say. How Leah would react if she knew he said anything.

"All I'm willing to say is that she could use a kind and gentle person in her life right now."

Tyler still didn't know the specifics, but he didn't have to. If Leah told him, fine. If she chose to keep it to herself and nothing ever happened between them again, he'd have to accept that. He'd focus on work and Maddie, go back to the man he was before Leah appeared in his life.

That seemed way emptier than it had before. Than it should be.

After he picked up Maddie from school and drove home, his niece unbuckled herself and ran into the house, unwilling to wait a moment longer to see Baxter.

"Can I take him to meet Felix?"

"I don't know if Leah wants company." Or maybe just not his.

"She said I could come by anytime."

What was he supposed to say that?

"Okay, but if she's busy, come right back."

"Are you going to come with me?"

He wanted to, a good deal more than the length of their acquaintance would suggest. But a person felt how they felt, no matter how irrational.

"Not today. I've got some work to do." Not a lie, but it wasn't as if the work was so pressing he couldn't spare a few minutes. But it felt as if he should leave Leah to make the next move, if she was going to.

He watched Maddie and Baxter until they reached the bunkhouse door. But when that door opened he turned away, afraid his desire to be with Leah again would override what she needed. And if what he'd gathered from her actions and Conner's answer was true and he ignored it, he'd be a selfish bastard. He'd rather live the rest of his life alone than have her think that of him or hurt her in any way.

However, he couldn't help but hope that it wouldn't come to that.

LEAH'S HEART JUMPED at the knock on the door, until she realized that it was much too small and faint to be Tyler. She wasn't sure if she was glad or disappointed Tyler wasn't the one at her door. She'd replayed the kiss between them over and over, not to mention India's words of advice. But how could she tell Tyler she was interested in him when she couldn't be sure that she wouldn't repeat how she'd jumped away from him? He'd managed to be gentle with her while also showing her the first flames of his desire. Remembering that stoked her own desire, and part of her wanted a replay. But the other part just wasn't sure.

If she hadn't figured it out after hours upon hours of thinking about it, she sure wasn't going to have an epiphany by making Maddie wait outside the door longer.

"Hey, sweetie," she said as she opened the door.

Immediately, Baxter ran past her feet into the bunkhouse, straight for where Felix was chewing on a rawhide bone in his fluffy new bed.

"Baxter, no!" Maddie called out as she also raced past Leah.

Whether it was Maddie's command or the realization that Felix was hurt, Baxter stopped suddenly and stared at Felix. For his part, Felix had stiffened and stared right back.

Maddie started to grab Baxter, but Leah stopped her by lightly gripping her shoulder.

"They're okay. Be gentle with Felix. His leg is broken."

"How did that happen?"

For a moment, Leah wondered how to answer, then decided on honesty. To a point, anyway. "Someone hurt him."

"Oh, poor Felix." She eased forward and sat beside Felix's bed.

At first, Felix just stared at Maddie's outstretched hand, faced with the decision of whether to trust once again. When he stood on his three good legs and nuzzled Maddie's hand, Leah's heart filled. Maddie was so gentle with Felix.

Sort of like Tyler had been with her.

She glanced toward the window, as if she could see him. Part of her yearned for it, to go back in time and not have pulled away from his kiss. India was right. She needed to embrace happiness and let it push out the fear.

Felix shifted his attention to Baxter when he barked one of his cute little puppy barks. Felix snuffed in response, making Maddie giggle and Leah smile.

"How about we take these two for a walk?"

"We can show Uncle Tyler that Baxter and Felix are best friends. I told him they would be."

Leah's heart sped up at the idea of seeing Tyler again, but hadn't that been the true reason for her suggestion for taking the pups for a walk? She couldn't help it. He was a marvelous man to look at, especially when she knew how his lips felt, his hands.

The sound of a horse's hooves drew Leah's attention as soon as they stepped outside. She looked to the right, toward the pasture that began beyond the gate at the end of the gravel drive. If she'd thought Tyler handsome before, the sight of him astride a horse took her breath away.

Maddie headed that way, Baxter running a bit ahead, yipping, then running back toward them. Felix moved at a slower pace.

When they reached the gate, Baxter nuzzled Felix's ear, as if asking if he was okay after an arduous journey.

Tyler spotted them and for a moment Leah thought he might pretend he hadn't. But then he reined the horse in their direction. Her heart beat faster the closer he came. As he stopped on the opposite side of the gate, his eyes met hers. She was so flustered and confused that she wasn't able to decipher what she saw there. But what she didn't see was anger. Could it be possible she was still seeing yearning, even after the way she'd reacted to the kiss?

"Look, Uncle Tyler. Baxter and Felix are best friends already."

Tyler shifted his attention to his niece. "Looks like you were right."

Maddie looked up at her uncle, who towered above her on Comet. "Can Leah eat dinner with us again?"

Tyler looked as surprised by the question as Leah was.

"Sure, if she wants to."

Yes, she did. How swift and certain the answer came to her told Leah all she needed to know. If Tyler made a second attempt to explore the attraction between them, she was going to try her hardest to go with it.

"Sure, but only if I can bring dessert."

Tyler smiled, making everything in her vibrate.

"Can't argue with that." He glanced down at Maddie then back at Leah. "Mind if squirt here stays with you for a little bit? I need to ride out and check a couple of things."

"Sure. She can help me bake the cake."

"Yay!" Maddie's enthusiasm was so sudden and loud that both puppies jumped, making everyone laugh.

When Tyler headed off toward his herd, Leah stood with her arms resting atop the gate, watching him until he rode out of sight.

"Come on, kiddo. We've got a cake to make."

Chapter Twelve

Maddie wiped the lemon icing off the butter knife then popped her icing-covered finger in her mouth. "Yum!"

Leah smiled at Maddie's reaction. It was so good to see the girl happy and building a relationship with her uncle. She never mentioned her mother, and Leah thought it was sad that Kendra had done such a poor job of parenting that her own daughter didn't even appear to miss her.

"Wash your hands so we can head down to the house."

"Okay." Maddie hopped up and ran to the bathroom.

Leah stared after her and didn't know what she'd do if the girl was ever not a part of her life. She didn't know what was going to happen with Tyler, but she hoped however that ended up she was still able to spend time with Maddie.

With Maddie in charge of the puppies, Leah grabbed the lemon cake and headed out the front door. As they approached Tyler's house, she grew more nervous. Already she was thinking ahead to the end of the evening, wondering if they might kiss again. This time she refused to let herself get spooked. Tyler was not Jason Garton.

At the smell of grilling meat, she changed her path from the front porch to the back deck instead.

"That smells great," she said as she, Maddie and the puppies rounded the back corner of the house.

Tyler looked up from where he was flipping a couple of steaks and a hot dog that she assumed was for Maddie. "I know. My stomach has been growling for the past ten minutes."

"I think mine is joining the chorus."

He pointed toward the cake container with his tongs. "Dessert, I take it."

For a moment, she was distracted by his nicely formed arm sticking out of a gray T-shirt. By the look of his still-damp hair, he'd showered since his ride out onto the ranch. She had the crazy idea that she wanted to sniff his fresh, clean scent.

"Uh, yeah," she said, remembering she was supposed to reply. "Lemon cake. I better put this inside." Before she started visibly drooling, and not because of the cake.

Once safely inside the house, she slid the cake onto the counter and looked around. She noticed the makings for a salad laid out and went to work. While part of her wanted to go back outside with Tyler, she needed time to calm down a little. It wasn't to be, however.

She kept her attention on peeling a cucumber as she listened to the door open and close, then the sound of Tyler's boots approaching.

"You don't have to do that."

"I don't mind. You're doing the hard part."

"Nah."

"I'm terrible at grilling."

Tyler leaned back against the counter close to her. "I guess you can't be good at everything."

She glanced up at him and saw with clarity that he wasn't talking about her jewelry making or even the cake he hadn't yet sampled. For all he knew, the cake tasted like sawdust. But he did know what her kiss tasted like, and he evidently wanted to let her know he liked it without crowding or pressing her. Was he telling her she hadn't run him off but that the next move had to be hers?

"I'm sorry about how I reacted." She hadn't intended to bring up the aborted kiss quite so soon, but the words just tumbled out.

"No need to apologize." Tyler moved to the stove, grabbing an oven mitt on the way, and pulled out two large, foil-wrapped potatoes. "I hope you like steak and potatoes. I didn't even ask."

"Sounds good to me." Just like his voice. As she watched him move about the kitchen, she realized she was falling for him. She didn't know if that was wise, but she didn't care. It wasn't as if she could decide not to. You couldn't change your feelings as easily as changing clothes.

Maddie came inside then, Felix in her arms and Baxter trotting along behind her. "I think Felix is tired."

Tyler turned and guided Maddie and the dogs out of the kitchen, leaving Leah standing there realizing she could get used to this, helping to make meals then sharing them with Tyler and Maddie. She imagined what it would be like to do this every day, every meal.

To keep from staring at Tyler during the meal, Leah

asked Maddie about school. Luckily, kindergarten was evidently an endless source of stories.

When they were done eating, Maddie asked if they could have cake.

"You have a big sweet tooth. Just like your…"

Leah noted the frozen look on Tyler's face and realized he'd been about to compare Maddie to her mother. His expression shifted to a forced smile.

"…uncle," he finished, then looked toward Leah. "I've been thinking of cake ever since you mentioned it earlier."

Nice recovery, but she also got the impression that when he looked at her it wasn't cake he was thinking about.

Her middle quivering, she stood and went to slice three pieces of cake.

"Uncle Tyler, do you like Leah?" Maddie asked right as Leah had turned back toward the table holding two small plates of cake.

Leah nearly dropped the plates.

"What?" Tyler asked in what sounded like shocked disbelief, as if Maddie had asked if she could take up skydiving.

"You watch her all the time, like Hannah does her boyfriend."

"Who is Hannah?"

"My neighbor at Mom's."

Leah watched, frozen, as Tyler's body stiffened at the mention of his sister.

"How old is Hannah?"

Maddie shrugged. "Sixteen, I think. She's in high school."

"Well, teenagers are different from adults."

"So you don't like Leah?"

How did this kid go from a virtual vow of silence to the Spanish Inquisition?

"I like Leah fine. Let's eat some cake."

Was that a blush staining Tyler's neck and face? Leah had the biggest urge to start laughing, but she managed to refrain. Instead, she brought the slices of cake and forks to the table then slid back onto her chair. She could feel the tension as she and Tyler tried not to look at each other.

"Do you like Uncle Tyler?" Maddie asked her.

"Maddie, stop," Tyler said. "Eat your cake."

Leah couldn't keep her gaze from Tyler any longer. She was dying to know what was going on in his head, if she could see any of it in his eyes. She decided to answer Maddie's question the same way Tyler had.

"I like him fine."

Tyler's gaze met hers, and she knew, deep down, that he was still interested every bit as much as she was. If not for Maddie's presence, Leah doubted she and Tyler would stay on opposite sides of the table for long.

At five years old, Maddie had no idea about the power and complexity of adult relationships, but she giggled nonetheless.

Leah pressed her lips together to keep from giggling, too.

AFTER FINALLY GETTING Maddie to sleep and leaving Baxter, her faithful companion, as her guard, Leah accompanied Tyler back downstairs. When they reached the living room and looked at each other, they both laughed.

"If she's this observant at five, I don't want to think about her teen years." Tyler paced over to the mantel and stopped in front of one of the pictures of him with Kendra. "I just hope I can keep her from making the types of dumb decisions Kendra did."

Leah walked up beside him and placed her hand on his arm. "Don't borrow trouble. Just enjoy the now."

He turned halfway toward her. "Sounds like my niece isn't the only smart person in the house tonight."

"Sometimes I don't feel so smart." She laced her hands together to keep from fidgeting. "Like when I pulled away from you when we kissed."

"I didn't move too fast?"

"No, and yes. Let's just say I wasn't expecting this when I moved to the bunkhouse."

"I didn't either. Getting involved with someone wasn't anywhere near the front of my mind."

"You have a lot of responsibilities and not a lot of free time, so that's understandable."

"But that's changed." He lifted his hand to her cheek and gently caressed it. "I haven't been able to stop thinking about that kiss."

Her heart soared. "That makes two of us."

"Can I kiss you, Leah?"

It seemed as if her heartbeat sped up and slipped into slow motion at the same time. "Yes."

Tyler closed the distance between them and framed her face between his large, powerful hands. But Leah didn't sense any danger from all that power he possessed. In fact, it was exactly the opposite, as if he was being deliberately gentle. Her heart swelled that he hadn't let her abrupt end to their first kiss convince him that she'd never want another.

"I won't hurt you," he said, as if he could read not only what she was thinking now but everything that led up to their first failed attempt.

"I know." And in this moment, she did know that. She just hoped the irrational part of her brain didn't decide to make another appearance.

As Tyler leaned toward her, her pulse went crazy. But it was with anticipation, not fear. When his lips made contact, she allowed herself to enjoy it fully, kissing him back and running her hands up his chest. Yes, there were definitely some very nice muscles under that T-shirt.

After a bit of kissing, Tyler deepened the kiss. It felt as if he was easing into it, probably afraid she'd balk. But this time, she didn't. Her fear didn't override her brain.

Tyler's hands slid to the back of her head, and he moaned as he pulled her closer still. The sound shot a surge of high-octane desire through Leah, and for the first time since the attack she thought she might really be able to enjoy desire and physical contact again.

She lost herself in the taste and feel of him, in the thrill of feeling more like herself again. She had no idea how much time had passed when Tyler was the one to pull away first. He ran his thumb softly across her cheek.

The sound of barely suppressed childish giggling drew their attention, causing them to quickly step back from each other. But when Leah saw Maddie sitting on the stairs, her mouth hidden behind her hands, it was obvious it didn't matter. The little stinker had seen them.

"I thought you were asleep," Tyler said as he crossed the living room and scooped her up into his arms.

"I was, for a little bit. You do like Leah. I knew it."

Tyler sighed and glanced toward Leah. "Yeah, squirt, I do."

"I do, too. You should get married."

Leah choked on a laugh at the same time as Tyler's mouth fell open.

"This town already has one matchmaker, missy." Tyler looked in Leah's direction, but didn't quite make eye contact. "I'll be back in a minute. I've got to go tie this one to her bed."

Maddie giggled and swatted Tyler playfully. "No, Uncle Tyler. I'll stay in bed. I promise."

"You better, or I'll eat the rest of that cake all by myself."

Leah smiled as she listened to Tyler tease Maddie all the way back up to her bedroom. She considered heading back to the bunkhouse, but she didn't relish the idea of going alone. She knew that if she continued to live there, she'd at some point have to get used to how dark the night was here without the glow of city lights. After all, all those city lights hadn't prevented her from being attacked.

But she had to admit she hoped Tyler would walk her back and they'd share some more kisses. But had Maddie's mention of marriage spooked him? It was definitely too early to be thinking of that, but Leah found she didn't mind the idea. She shook her head and took a few steps toward the door as she heard Tyler on the stairs.

"You ready to call it a night?" Tyler asked as he reached the bottom of the stairs.

"Yeah. But I had a lovely evening. Thanks for inviting me."

"You're welcome anytime."

That was a good sign. At least she believed he was sincere, that Maddie's mention of the *M* word hadn't doused his interest.

Leah's heart started racing again as they stepped outside and Tyler took her hand in his. How long had it been since she'd held hands with a guy, someone she really liked? Ages. It felt so wonderful that she nearly cried. Instead, she looked up at the sky filled to bursting with stars.

"It's like an entirely different world out here."

Tyler stopped and looked up, too. "I remember Kendra and I would come outside in the summer and chase fireflies. When we got tired, we'd lie in the grass and watch for shooting stars. I miss how things were then."

"She's still young. Maybe she'll turn her life around."

"I used to hope that, but I got to the point where I'd been disappointed one too many times. I have to look forward to what's best for Maddie." He lowered his gaze to Leah's. "And me."

He kissed her again, and the fact they were kissing beneath such a beautiful night sky, far from the place and thoughts that had haunted her for weeks, filled her with hope for her own future, too.

WHEN TYLER WENT to pick up Maddie from school the next day, she came running out all smiles and unbound childhood excitement.

"Uncle Tyler, Helena is having a birthday party at

her house Saturday. Everyone is spending the night.
Can I go? Pretty please!"

"Who is Helena?"

She pointed back toward the school building to
where a little girl with dark curls was walking hand
in hand with her mom toward them. He recognized
the woman as Janie Larned, who'd been behind him
in school by a couple of years. Except she was Janie
Struthers now. He'd shoed a couple of horses for Janie
and her husband, Blake, last year.

Janie smiled when she saw him and Maddie. "I'm
guessing she's asking about the slumber party."

"Yeah. First thing out of her mouth."

"We'd love to have her. The girls will be well super-
vised."

He smoothed Maddie's hair. "Then I guess it's
okay."

Maddie and Helena jumped up and down squeal-
ing. Sometimes he couldn't believe Maddie was the
same child who had been left with him not so long
ago. And he had Leah to thank for that.

And for awakening something in him he hadn't realized had been ignored for way too long. The need
to connect with someone else.

As he drove home, the reality that Maddie would
be gone overnight revealed possibilities to him. He
could ask Leah out on a real date, not just a meal that
she helped to prepare. He thought about taking her
to Austin for a night out, but that was too far in case
Maddie needed him. She was only now getting used
to living with him. Would she get homesick? Plus,
there were the puppies to consider.

"You should give Leah flowers," Maddie said out

of the blue from the other side of the truck. "Girls like flowers."

"They do?"

She nodded. "Yep."

"You seem to know a lot about what girls like."

She gave him a "duh" look. "Because I'm a girl."

He laughed. "That you are." A little girl he couldn't love any more if she were his own daughter.

He knew it was time he consulted an attorney about making her living with him permanent. He was scared to bring up the topic, afraid it would prompt officials to ask too many questions, ones that could lead to them taking her away from him. He gripped the steering wheel harder. He couldn't let that happen, but avoiding the topic wasn't sustainable long-term. He needed a legal way to keep her from having to go back into a dangerous and unstable environment with her mother if Kendra were to pop back into her life without any notice.

But he couldn't do anything about that right now. He could, however, make plans to be with the woman who was coming to mean more to him every day.

Chapter Thirteen

Leah looked yet again at the text message Tyler had sent her two days before, the latest in a string of countless rereadings.

Don't plan anything for Saturday.

He hadn't told her why when she'd asked, not even a clue. So, of course as Saturday dawned, she hadn't been able to sleep a wink more. She knew from Maddie that she was going to be gone to a friend's birthday festivities until tomorrow. That meant Leah could be alone with Tyler. Excitement and anxiety had been bombarding her in equal measure since that information bomb had landed.

Even more so now that she heard Tyler's truck coming back up the driveway. Maddie was off playing with other kindergartners, and Leah's true test of how well she'd moved past her attack was on the verge of beginning. She pressed a hand against her churning stomach.

"Stop. I want to enjoy this."

Her stomach ignored her.

With each minute that passed, she paced more and

more. If she kept this up, she was going to have to pay for new flooring.

Her phone buzzed where she'd placed it on the table next to a red-and-silver necklace she couldn't concentrate enough on to finish. She picked up the phone, wondering if it was another cryptic message from Tyler.

Come to the barn.

At least he was somewhat more specific this time. What was he going to do, teach her to shoe a horse so she had a fallback career plan?

With her nerves seemingly having taken up Irish step dancing, she headed out the door and down the driveway. When she entered the barn, Tyler stood there next to Comet. She noticed the horse was saddled.

"We're going for a ride?" she asked.

"I thought we might. It's a pretty day for one."

"I'm not a very accomplished rider." She rubbed Comet's nose, smiling when he sniffed her.

"Lucky for you I am."

The idea of sitting pressed next to Tyler sent a surge of pure animal awareness through her. After he helped her mount then swung up behind her, she thought she might combust before they even left the barn.

As he brought his arms around her to grip the reins, he leaned close to her ear. "Relax."

Yeah, right. That wasn't happening anytime soon.

Tyler steered Comet toward the gate to the pasture. He dismounted only long enough to open the gate, guide the horse through and refasten the gate. Then he was right back in the saddle, snug against Leah's bottom. And it was obvious that his position was having an effect on him. Jitters danced through her. She had to get her mind on something else.

"So, was Maddie still as excited about the sleepover today as she was yesterday?"

"You could say that. I think she's making up for all those weeks she barely spoke."

"But you don't mind one bit."

"No, I don't. She can talk my ears off if she wants to."

Leah wrapped her hand around his lower arm. "You're a good man, Tyler. She's lucky to have you."

"And you. If not for you, she might still be trapped in that shell of hers."

"You don't know that. She probably just had to get comfortable here, used to you. It was a big change for her."

"Yeah, maybe. But the truth is that once she began hanging out with you, she started to change back into the child I remembered."

"I'm happy for you both."

They rode in silence for a few minutes, broken only when Tyler would point out something of interest. A neighbor's house in the distance. The spot where he fell off his first horse and broke his arm. The tree under which his father sat him down to tell him about the birds and the bees.

"I thought he was crazy when he said someday I'd really like girls. Turns out he was right."

Tyler reined in Comet, causing Leah to look over her shoulder at him. His lips claimed hers in a kiss so hot that she found herself surrendering to it gladly. He tasted like coffee, rich and dark and delicious.

When he lifted his mouth, he smiled, looking pleased with himself. "Yep, dear old Dad was right."

They rode across the ranch a while longer before Tyler turned Comet back toward the barn. When they reached it, he had to help Leah dismount.

She stretched her arms above her head then bent to touch her toes. "Ow. I'm going to regret this tomorrow."

"I hope not too much," Tyler said as he removed Comet's saddle.

"Well, not the ride or the company, but the soreness afterward, most definitely. I'll be lucky if I can walk." A very naughty image popped into her head. As she felt the heat rush to her face like water coming from a fire hose, she walked toward the opposite end of the barn, acting like she was simply working out the kinks.

"You okay?"

Without turning or saying anything, she extended a thumbs-up over her shoulder. When she reached the end of the barn that looked out over the pasture, she stopped and took in the view. It really was a beautiful place. She heard Tyler's approaching footsteps.

"You're lucky you grew up here," she said when he stepped up next to her.

"Yeah. I've never wanted to live anywhere else. Did you not like growing up in Houston?"

"I liked it fine. I mean, it's all I knew. Though I always liked coming to Blue Falls to visit Conner and his family." Worried that he might ask her why she'd decided to move there after living her entire life in

Houston, she turned to him. "All that riding made me hungry. I can throw together something if you're hungry, too."

He smiled. "I already have that covered. Stay here. I'll be right back."

After Tyler hurried out of the barn, Leah strolled back to the other end where she could see him eating up the ground to the house with his long legs. He was inside less than a minute before he came back out carrying a picnic basket.

"Aren't you full of surprises," she said.

When he got close, he extended his arm and she took it.

"I thought we'd eat by the creek. Have you been down there yet?"

"I have. It's a lovely little oasis."

"The perfect swimming hole when you're a kid and it's scorching hot outside."

As they walked toward the creek, Leah couldn't help but imagine Tyler swimming in that cool water, but not as a boy. As a man, the water running down over his bare chest. She stumbled, but Tyler steadied her as if it were no more difficult than holding a butterfly on the end of his finger.

"Sorry," she said. "I seem to always be tripping over my own feet."

"Should I take that as a compliment?"

"More that I'm klutzy."

When they reached the side of the creek, Tyler pulled a blanket from the basket and spread it out on the ground. When he began to pull out containers of food, including a bottle of wine with scrolling wildflowers covering the label, she sank beside the basket to help him.

"Where did you get all this?"

"The Primrose, except for the wine. It's bottled at a winery on the other side of the county."

She ran her fingers across the beautiful label. "Blue Falls really is making the most of diversifying for the tourist trade."

"It's good for the local economy."

"I heard they're going to launch an arts and crafts trail. That should bring in a lot of people, too."

"Seems there is something new starting every day. And not just in town."

She looked up and met his eyes. He leaned forward and gifted her with a soft, sweet kiss.

"That's a nice appetizer," she said.

"Yes, it is."

Before she let herself get carried away, she sat back and finished pulling napkins and utensils from the basket. "Did you buy the basket, too?"

"No, that was my mom's. It's been around as long as I can remember. We used to picnic down here, all four of us."

"That sounds like a nice memory."

He nodded then looked at her. "This will be, too."

As they ate, they shared stories of their childhoods, how they both liked working for themselves with the freedom to make their own decisions, and about how the creek was indeed fed by a spring.

She was amazed by how easy it was to talk to Tyler, to be alone with him without being afraid. Compared with her state upon arrival at the ranch, it seemed like nothing less than a miracle.

As the sun set, their little oasis took on a twilit glow. It looked like a place right out of a fairy tale. Which seemed appropriate because her entire day with Tyler had seemed like one.

"Penny for your thoughts."

She smiled. "I think that saying is seriously in need of revision for inflation."

Tyler smiled, too, and smoothed a tendril of her hair at her temple. It was such a simple touch, but she felt it throughout her entire body.

"Thank you for today," she said. "It was wonderful."

"It's not over yet." The look in his eyes seemed to be asking permission. For what, she wasn't sure.

Even so, she leaned forward, initiating the kiss this time. Tyler's arms came around her, pulling her close. They kissed for several minutes, so long that night began to fall around them.

"I like being with you," Tyler said as he pressed his forehead to hers.

"I feel the same." She did, but the encroaching darkness was causing a layer of unease to rise within her. Even though she'd been with Tyler all day and should feel safe with him, there was something about the night that caused her fear to crawl out from where it had been hiding like some nocturnal animal, one bent on sinking its big teeth into her.

Tyler captured her lips in a sweet, soft kiss that made her temporarily forget the looming fear but was over much too quickly. Then he stood and extended his hand to her. He didn't say anything to that effect, but she felt as if he knew how much the dark bothered her but didn't question it. She shouldn't be surprised. He was a smart man, and she'd given him ample evidence.

Though she'd been adamant about no one else knowing about her attack, feeling like the more people who knew the more the memories would linger, she suddenly wanted to explain to him. She didn't want him to think her fear had anything to do with him because she…cared for him a great deal.

But she didn't start spilling her story. Instead, she helped him repack the picnic basket then folded up the blanket.

"Let's get up the path while we can still see how," he said.

His words made perfect sense, and yet she suspected there was so much more going on inside his head.

He took her hand as they climbed the path and crossed the driveway back to the front of the bunkhouse. The first stars of the evening began to wink on against the darkening sky.

"Thanks for spending the day with me," Tyler said.

A surge of panic welled up in Leah, nearly choking her. But it wasn't because she feared him or what he might do to her. Rather, she grasped for some reason to make him stay because she wanted that more than anything. She realized that with every moment she'd spent with him over the past several hours, she'd fallen for him a bit more until her heart was fully involved. She didn't want the day to end, hated the idea of going into the bunkhouse alone while Tyler went back to his house.

She didn't think she was the only one who'd had similar thoughts. But was she healed enough, strong enough to take things further, for them to not spend their night in separate beds?

"Would you like to come in?"

Even with night upon them, she still saw the way he looked at her, as if conflicting feelings were tugging him in two directions. He lifted the hand not holding the picnic basket and gently caressed the side of her face.

"I think we should say good-night here."

No! The single word screamed inside her. After such a wonderful day, going inside alone held no appeal at all.

"What if I don't want to?"

The way he looked at her, with a sadness that could have no other source, gave her a sinking feeling in her middle.

"You know, don't you?"

He didn't answer immediately, hesitating as if trying to formulate an answer. She detected a slight sigh leaving him into the night air.

"I don't know what, but I can tell there is something that frightens you. Or someone. And it's made worse by the dark."

"So Conner didn't tell you?"

He shook his head. "But I'll be honest, I did ask him."

She jerked back in shock. "Why?"

"Because I hated the idea of you being hurt, and I wanted to know if I needed to protect you."

"That isn't your job. You're my landlord."

"I hope I'm more than that. I consider us friends, at least."

At least? Just how far did his feelings extend? Were

they on similar paths as far as that went? The fact that she was contemplating having him spend the night said better than words could just how her feelings for him had changed.

"We are…at least that."

He took her hand and squeezed it gently. "I won't lie and say I don't want more, but I'm not the kind of man who will push a woman. I've waited this long. I can wait longer."

She slipped her hand from his and crossed her arms across her chest as she faced the blanket of darkness back toward the creek, her mind racing. This felt like one of those pivotal moments in her life that she'd look back on when she was old and gray. She didn't want to look back on it with regret.

Cold chills broke out across her skin as the memory of that night washed over her. But if she wanted to move forward with Tyler, she had to tell him. How else would she be able to explain if her irrational fear overwhelmed her again in a passionate moment?

Unable to look at him as she spoke, she kept her gaze pointed ahead, at what now looked like a solid black canvas.

"I was attacked in my apartment back in Houston. A man I didn't know broke in and was waiting for me when I got home one night after visiting my parents. I know he planned to jump me in the dark, but I flipped on the light a bit quicker than he anticipated. I know because I saw the surprised look on his face a fraction of a second before he grabbed me and clamped a hand over my mouth. He turned the light back off and dragged me to my couch."

Tyler stood perfectly still, not saying a word. The

fact that he seemed to know not to interrupt or she might not get through the telling made her heart open to him even more.

"Sometimes I would swear I can still feel his hands on my skin. They were heavy, clammy." She shuddered at the memory. "He pawed at me, trying to get my clothes off while keeping one hand on my mouth. His grip slipped and I started screaming and knocked some containers of beads off my coffee table, sending them spilling in all directions. That's when…" Her voice faltered, but she pushed on. She had to get through the entire story before her scraped-together courage abandoned her.

"He clamped his hand around my throat, and I thought for sure he would choke me to death. That's why I jumped away from the kiss that night. Your hand grazed my neck, and suddenly I was right back on that couch, afraid I was going to be raped or killed or both."

She sensed Tyler was about to apologize, but she held up a hand to forestall him.

"It wasn't your fault, and you couldn't have known. I know it was an irrational reaction. You're not him. But ever since that night, I've been so nervous to be around men not related to me. And the dark. The fear of what might be lurking in the dark, ready to attack, is so overwhelming it's hard to even function."

She dared a glance at Tyler and saw a mixture of sympathy and anger on his handsome face. Though she hadn't known him all that long, she knew that anger was not directed at her but at Jason Garton and what he'd done to her.

"That's why you were so scared the night you ran from your car and fell outside the barn," he said.

She nodded. "I felt like a fool, but out in the darkness the danger felt very real, like if I slowed down even the tiniest bit whoever was after me would catch me." She took a breath, still not quite able to believe she was sharing all this with Tyler. What if he thought she was stark raving mad?

Well, at least she'd know before she passed the point of no return with him.

"Please tell me the bastard is rotting in jail."

"He is. I managed to hit him and slip away as the cops arrived. One of my neighbors heard me screaming, and luckily I lived close to a police precinct. It was literally two blocks away. Even so, and knowing he was behind bars, I never felt safe in my home again. I wasn't sleeping, barely eating, not able to work. I knew if I was going to get back on a good path, I had to make a big change." She looked at him and half smiled. "And that's how I ended up here."

Tyler took two slow steps toward her and gently gripped her shoulders. "I hate what happened to you, but I'm glad you're here."

She was, too. She wasn't sure if she believed in destiny, but it certainly felt as if she'd made the right choice moving to the ranch. Being with Maddie and Tyler had helped her begin to heal, but she suspected she would have loved them anyway.

Love? Did she love Tyler? A voice inside her, one that belonged to her heart, said yes. And it didn't say it in a whisper. Especially after what had happened, how could she possibly have fallen in love so quickly? Was she confusing gratitude for love?

As she looked up into Tyler's eyes, she knew what she was feeling wasn't gratitude. It was desire stemming from the fact that she loved him. That frightened her in an entirely different way, the kind that created a fear of loss. She shoved that thought away. This had been a perfect day, and she wanted to add a perfect night.

"I don't want you to go," she said, her voice thick with emotion.

"I don't want to, either."

"Then stay."

Leah took his strong hand in hers and led him inside, his strength and powerful presence allowing her to walk into the dark interior of the bunkhouse without fear.

It was Tyler who turned on the light before pulling her into his arms and capturing her mouth in a kiss that felt as if it might consume her but in the best way possible.

When he took a moment to breathe, he gently framed her face. "Are you sure about this, Leah? I don't want to do anything to frighten you."

She hesitated a moment then nodded. "What I'm most afraid of is never getting past being afraid. If what happened to me hadn't happened, I wouldn't even hesitate right now." In fact, she suspected they'd already be in the bedroom, ripping off each other's clothes.

"I want this, too, but I will stop if you need me to."

She reached up and placed her palm against his warm cheek, felt the slight bristle of whiskers that had appeared since he'd shaved that morning.

"I know." She looked into his eyes and hoped with

all her heart that he felt the same way about her as she did him. "Kiss me, Tyler."

He did, with a thoroughness that made her head spin. He wrapped his arms around her and pulled her close. She was relieved that the action, which put her at his mercy, didn't freak her out. Her heart sped up as Tyler started backing her toward her bedroom, but it was in anticipation. Everywhere he touched, her skin came alive.

When they reached the side of her bed, Tyler didn't press her. Instead, he continued to kiss her, melting any resistance that might have still existed within her. Though it was obvious he desired her, he took care with her, making her love him even more.

Deciding she needed to make the first move, she slid her hands underneath his shirt. Tyler's sharp intake of breath told her that the feel of her hands against his taut stomach thrilled him every bit as much as it did her. She moved her hands farther up and over his chest, liking what she found.

Tyler's mouth came down on hers with an intensity he'd not yet shown. Still, her fear miraculously stayed away. Growing more excited, she kissed him back with enough energy that she hoped it said without words that she was ready to move beyond kissing.

In the next moment, Tyler scooped her up into his arms, causing her to yelp in surprise.

"You okay?" he asked, a look of concern on his face.

She smiled. "Better than I've been in a long time."

Slowly, as if he thought she'd still change her mind, Tyler laid her on the bed, then stretched out beside her. He didn't immediately kiss her again but rather caressed her cheek with his fingertip.

"You're so beautiful."

Her heart sang, full and high and free. "And you are very easy on the eyes yourself."

He smiled wide. "That right?"

"Yes," she said.

At first, he kissed her gently, but their kisses grew deeper and more urgent. When Tyler's hands made contact with the bare skin of her stomach, she flinched instinctively. But the feeling passed as her rational brain kicked the fear to some dark corner.

Tyler started to pull back, but she grasped his shoulder and held him close. "No, I want this."

He didn't look convinced, so she tugged at the bottom of his shirt. When she had it up to his arms, he stared down at her for a moment before pulling the shirt the rest of the way off and tossing it back over his shoulder.

She giggled. "With moves like that, I feel like I need to have some stripper music at the ready."

His eyes widened. "I can't believe you just said that."

She shrugged. "It was an impressive move."

"You say that like you've seen strippers."

"There may have been a trip to a certain club for Reina's bachelorette party."

"I'm afraid I don't have those kinds of moves."

She ran her hand slowly up his chest. "That's not what I want."

The truth was Tyler had all those strippers beat by a dozen miles in the looks department. In fact, if there was a better-looking man in all of Texas, she'd never met him. When she felt how his heart was beating against her hand, it shot her desire for him into overdrive. She grabbed the bottom of her own shirt and removed it quickly, tossing it in the general direction of Tyler's.

With a hungry growl, Tyler captured her mouth and kissed her thoroughly, moving cautiously to her throat, probably afraid she'd balk.

"I'm okay," she said.

His lips and tongue kept moving south. She felt his hands at her back and then her bra unclasping before he captured her right breast in his mouth. Raw, pulsing need shot through her, had her grasping for his belt buckle.

The pace picked up, and soon they were both naked. After Tyler turned away long enough to put on a condom, they kissed and caressed and explored with their hands, their mouths, their tongues. She wanted Tyler so much that she thought she might burst from the wanting. He seemed to be feeling the same, but he still looked into her eyes as he nudged her legs apart with his knee, watching for any sign that she wanted to stop. But she didn't. She wanted him to keep going, and she told him so by entwining her fingers with his where his hands were braced above her head and spreading her legs to welcome him.

Tyler eased into her, perhaps still not convinced she wouldn't stop him. But when he slid all the way in, his eyes closed as if he were savoring the feel of her surrounding him. Without even thinking about it, she moved to create more friction. With a very male sound deep in his throat, Tyler began to move, each stroke slightly faster than the one before.

Leah's breath started to come in pants, and she gripped Tyler's shoulders as if she might fly away if she didn't. The pleasure coursing through her body built until she was close to exploding. Tyler was beautiful. She wouldn't tell him that using that term, but he was, and not just physically. Her love for him grew right alongside the pleasure he was giving her.

The muscles inside her tensed and then the rest of the ones throughout her body as she plunged over the edge into glorious release. As if he'd been holding back until she reached her peak, Tyler quickly followed.

One moment he was rigidly tense all over, and in the next his muscles seemed to lose their ability to support him and he sank down beside her. But he still had the strength to wrap his arm around her and pull her close. She nestled next to him as if it were the most natural action for her to take. And it strangely seemed so.

"Are you okay?" he asked, his breath warm against the top of her head.

She ran her fingertips up his chest. "Way better than okay." Tears stung her eyes. "I feel like I've broken free of a cage I put myself in." She leaned back so she could look up at him. "I'm happy. So very happy."

He kissed her with a sweetness that belied his size and the power he could command at a moment's notice. But his size and strength didn't scare her anymore, which felt like a miracle. In fact, as she snuggled against him, bare in more ways than one, she felt safer than she had since before the attack.

As she drifted toward satisfied sleep, she hoped that this wasn't a one-time thing. If she were being honest, she wanted this for the rest of her life.

Chapter Fourteen

Tyler resisted the urge to kiss Leah's soft lips as she lay on his arm sleeping. She looked so peaceful in the early morning light, he didn't want to wake her. He suspected this had been the first really good night of sleep she'd gotten since the attack.

Just the idea that some man had pawed at her like an animal, making her fear for her life, causing her so much trauma, made him want to rip the guy's head from his body. But he would never tell Leah that. By some miracle, she'd trusted him enough to be with him in the most intimate way, so he wasn't going to repay her by sharing his violent thoughts.

As he watched her sleep, his heart felt content, like he'd be perfectly happy to stay here with her forever. What exactly did that mean? Was he falling in love with her? It certainly felt like it. Did she feel the same? He found himself hoping so, and that he wasn't just another stepping-stone on her path to healing. He wished he could say he was strong enough to be okay with that, but it would be a lie. Once he'd started developing feelings for her, they had deepened quickly, like a stone dropped into the middle of the lake.

Felix whimpered from the living room, which was followed by the sound of his uneven gait.

Leah stirred beside him. "He has to go potty."

Tyler did lean over and kiss her forehead then. "Stay here. I'll take him out." He slid from the bed and pulled on his jeans.

"It's a shame to cover that up," Leah said, her voice still tinged with sleep.

He glanced over his shoulder. "Like the view, huh?"

"Mmm-hmm."

Damn if he didn't go instantly hard at that appreciative sound in her throat. Were it not for a puppy about to piddle on the floor, he'd be back in that bed with her in the blink of an eye.

Instead, he left the room and headed straight for the front door. "Come on, little guy."

As Felix did his business, Tyler's gaze landed on the wildflowers growing along the opposite side of the driveway and remembered Maddie's assertion that girls liked flowers. He let Felix sniff about the bunkhouse's small yard as he picked a bouquet. He didn't think he'd ever actually picked flowers for anyone before, but it felt right.

"What do you think, boy? Will she like them?" he asked Felix, who cocked his head a bit to the side as if wondering why the crazy man would be asking a dog his opinion about flowers.

He half expected Leah to be up when he walked back inside, but after putting the flowers in water in a glass, he found her right where he'd left her.

She looked at him through her barely opened eyes. "I don't want to get up. I can't remember the last time I've felt this comfortable."

Tyler slid back into the bed with her. "That's the good thing about being your own boss. You can make your own hours."

"You make an excellent point." She rolled toward him, the sheet falling away to reveal the swell of her breasts. "What time do you have to pick up Maddie?"

"Not till noon."

She smiled. "Best news I've heard all day."

"I aim to please."

Leah's hand slid over his hip. "That you do."

He kissed her hard, much more so than he'd been willing to do the night before for fear of frightening her and bringing back horrible memories. Leah responded in kind, and soon they were making love again. They lay tangled together afterward, kissing, until he couldn't put off getting up and ready so he could pick up Maddie on time.

Leah tossed on her discarded T-shirt and rounded the bed where he stood fastening his pants for the second time that morning. She took his hands when he was done and held them in her own.

"Thank you for last night," she said.

He knew she'd enjoyed herself every bit as much as he had, but for her it had been so much more.

"You're welcome, though I feel as if I should be the one thanking you."

"Really?"

"Why do you sound so surprised?"

"I don't know, but I am. Or do you usually thank women for sex?"

Her question startled him. "I don't recall, maybe because it's been so long." He smoothed her hair, mussed by sleep and sex. "Last night wasn't just sex for me, Leah."

He watched as she swallowed and her eyes took on a glow that tugged at his heart.

"It wasn't?"

"I care about you, more than ought to be possible at this point. I didn't expect it or plan for it, but do anyway."

"Tyler." She seemed at a loss for what to say other than his name, so he lifted her from her feet and kissed her.

As he stood with Leah at the bunkhouse door a couple of minutes later, it startled him how much he didn't want to leave her.

"Come meet me and Maddie at the Primrose for lunch."

The past twenty-four hours had been so great that he kept expecting the bubble to burst, expected it to be now when she declined.

"Okay."

It took Tyler a moment to realize that she hadn't replied the way he thought she would. But the fact that she'd accepted made him grin like a fool. After another lingering kiss, he headed down the driveway toward his house for a shower and clean clothes.

He was halfway there before he realized he was whistling.

WHEN LEAH WALKED into the Primrose Café right after noon, she felt as if everyone in the building would take one look at her and know what she'd done with Tyler the night before. As if "I had awesome sex last night!" was blinking in bright lights across her forehead.

She spotted a table in the middle of the dining area and headed for it. She'd barely seated herself before the waitress stopped by with a menu.

When she heard the door open, she somehow knew it was Tyler before she even turned to look. His smile when their eyes met made her tingle all over and remember every single touch they'd shared during their night together. That he'd asked her to lunch and looked happy to see her now suggested he wasn't having any day-after regrets. And neither was she. In addition to the great sex and the tenderness he'd shown her, she'd slept solid and without interruption. It was as if all the sleep she'd missed out on since the attack had found her. It was huge that she'd felt safe enough with him to sleep that soundly.

"Hey, Leah," Maddie said as she hurried toward the table. "Look, I got a tattoo." Maddie stuck out her arm to show Leah her temporary pink-and-purple butterfly tattoo on her forearm.

"Why, yes, you do. Very pretty."

"It's not real."

"That's good, because you might get tired of the butterfly and want something else."

"Don't encourage tattoos," Tyler said. "At least not until she's, oh, thirty."

"Did you have fun at the party?" Leah asked.

"Yes!" And she proceeded to tell Leah everything she and her new friends had done, pausing only long enough to tell the waitress she wanted chicken nuggets.

Leah glanced across the table at Tyler, and he was having a difficult time not smiling. She wondered if he was hearing all of Maddie's stories for the second time.

"Did you and Uncle Tyler have fun on your date? Did he bring you flowers? I told him to."

He'd told her about their day?

"Uh, we had a nice time. We went for a horseback ride and had a picnic. And yes, he brought me flowers." Which she'd discovered that morning after he'd left.

Thank goodness their food arrived then, but so did India Parrish.

"Hey, guys," India said.

After a round of hellos, India turned to Leah. "I was just chatting with Gina this morning, so the arts and crafts trail is fresh on my mind. Have you thought any more about whether you might take part?"

"I don't know. I'm still getting settled, and I'm not sure I want people coming and going."

"Okay," India said, sounding surprised by Leah's answer. "I understand, but I hope you change your mind."

After India left, Tyler said, "Maybe you should do it. The exposure would be good for your business. And meeting new people might be nice, too."

She met his gaze and thought she understood where he was coming from, that maybe she should open herself up to more people in order to continue healing.

"Maybe just one day a week, and I could make sure I'm around that day in case you need any help," he said.

Or protection. She knew that's what he really meant but didn't want to say in front of Maddie or within earshot of the other restaurant customers.

Should she do it? Could she? Yes, she'd been fine with Tyler the night before, but he was someone she cared about deeply. She felt safe with him because he'd shown her he could be trusted. But she wouldn't know the people who would come through her door. The idea of inviting strangers into her home threatened to resurrect her panic.

"I'll think about it," she said, mainly so they could move on to another topic of conversation.

Later that night, after Maddie was tucked away in bed, Leah sat with Tyler on his front steps enjoying a cooler breeze blowing ahead of a thunderstorm rolling in from the west.

"I've got an appointment with an attorney tomorrow to see what I need to do to gain custody of Maddie," Tyler said after they'd been sitting quietly, holding hands, for a few minutes.

"That's good," she said. "Maddie really has come alive here. It seems to be a good place for that."

"I just want you both to be happy and safe. I'll do whatever I have to in order to ensure that."

She wanted so much to tell him that she loved him then, but something held her back. Maybe the fear that this would all somehow be ripped away from her, that it was temporary. Plus, guys were weird about those three little words. It had taken Jacob forever and a day to tell Reina he loved her. Leah had begun to wonder if he really did when he'd finally said the words Reina had been dying to hear.

"What I said today about you being part of the arts and crafts trail, I meant it. I was thinking we could even convert one of the bedrooms into a little shop and put an exterior entrance to it so that no one has to come through your personal space."

"I don't know. Part of me likes the idea, but I'm not sure if I'm ready for that."

He wrapped his arm around her shoulders and pulled her close. "Whenever you are, just let me know."

She leaned back and looked up at him.

"What?" he asked.

"My life has changed so much since I moved here, all for the better. I'm afraid I'm going to wake up to find it's all been a dream."

He cupped her face and lowered his mouth close to hers. "It's not a dream."

Then he kissed her, and something about the kiss was different from any they'd shared before. It felt... more important, filled with deeper feelings. Or was that only wishful thinking on her part?

When he broke the kiss, he leaned his forehead against hers. "I want you so much right now."

"But we can't with Maddie here."

"I don't want to do anything that could jeopardize my chances of becoming her legal guardian. I know there's no one around, but—"

"You don't have to explain. I totally understand and agree with you."

But when she locked the door behind her at the bunkhouse, it seemed so empty without him.

LEAH HUMMED ALONG to the song playing on the grocery store's sound system as she made her way up the pasta aisle. It took a remarkable amount of willpower to keep from adding some dance moves to the mix.

"You certainly sound happy."

Leah turned to see India smiling at her. "Are you stalking me? Everywhere I go, there you are. I didn't see people in my apartment building in Houston as much as I see you."

India laughed. "One of the perils of small-town life."

"Another thing to get used to."

"Seems you're getting used to Tyler pretty well."

Leah thought about brushing India's observation off but realized she didn't want to. "He's a very kind man."

"For whom you have feelings."

Leah nodded. "I do."

India smiled as she leaned forward to hug Leah. "I'm happy for you."

"I don't know if it's going anywhere." She was afraid to allow herself to think too far ahead.

"Hon, none of us know that when we first get involved with someone. We just take it day by day."

"I guess you're right."

"Just go with it if it feels right. After what you've been through, I'd say it's a positive sign if you're comfortable with Tyler."

That's what Leah had been thinking, but it was nice to have the same thing said by someone not involved in the situation.

India's words played over and over in Leah's head as she drove home. Sometime recently when she'd not really been paying attention, she'd started thinking of the ranch as her home. Even Tyler's house was feeling more that way with as much time as she was spending there having meals, watching Maddie while

Tyler went out on a couple of jobs, watching movies, playing games and engaging in some mighty excellent kissing. She'd been there to comfort him when he'd second-guessed himself after meeting with the attorney about becoming Maddie's guardian.

She and Tyler had also made love a couple of more times, but always while Maddie was at school. It felt decadent to be in bed with Tyler in the middle of the day when they both should be working. They'd even let time get away from them one day and had still been naked when a customer had arrived with a couple of horses he needed shoed. Leah had giggled as Tyler raced to get his clothes on.

He still hadn't mentioned anything about love, but she was content with how things were between them. It felt safe and thrilling at the same time.

She made the turn into the ranch, remembering how foreign everything had felt the night she'd run to the ranch from her car. Now the turn brought her the happiness of coming home to a place and people she loved.

Her smile disappeared when she pulled within view of the house and saw Tyler and another man fighting in the front yard.

"Oh, my God!" She hit the accelerator and sped the rest of the way then skidded to a stop beside Tyler's truck. Fear rushed up within her, making her shake, but she had to help Tyler. He was a big guy, but the other man wasn't small. And he looked mean. Already she could see blood on Tyler's face.

As she forced herself out of her car, she dialed 911 on her phone, telling the dispatcher she was Conner's cousin in case that helped get the sheriff's department out to the ranch faster, before something truly horrible happened.

She felt so helpless, and bile rose in her throat and chills broke out all over her body when she remembered the last time she'd felt like this. Refusing to let it overwhelm her again, she picked up a large piece of gravel. When the other man tripped Tyler, she threw the rock with all her strength. Though she'd been aiming for the unknown man's head, she hit only a glancing blow to the back of his neck. But it was enough to draw his attention.

"Stupid bitch." He made only one step toward her before Leah saw the fury on Tyler's face a moment before he kicked the guy in the side of his knee, taking him down with a howl.

"No, I don't want to go!"

Leah's attention shot to the front of the house where a thin woman was dragging Maddie down the steps. The sound of the girl's hysterical crying broke something free inside Leah, something primal and fierce, willing to do whatever was necessary to protect Maddie.

Having to trust that Tyler could hold his own, Leah stalked toward the woman. "Let her go!"

The woman who looked at Leah was Kendra, a version that had obviously lived hard judging by the lines on her face, the dark circles under her eyes and the way her body barely looked strong enough to carry her own thin frame let alone drag a crying, resisting child against her will.

"Who the hell are you?"

"Someone who isn't going to let you hurt Maddie anymore. You've put her through enough."

Maddie used her mother's distraction against her and broke free. She ran straight to Leah, and she pulled her close then behind her so she could act as a shield between mother and child. Over all of the commotion, Leah could hear Baxter and Felix going crazy barking inside the house.

Kendra pointed at Leah with a bony finger. "You give her back to me."

"No."

Anger contorted what had once been a pretty face, could be again if Kendra would just turn her life around. "No? You have no right to deny me my child."

"I do if I think her life is in danger. You're not fit to take care of yourself, let alone a child."

"You're the one who did it, aren't you? Made my own brother try to take my baby girl away from me?"

"You did that all by yourself. Maddie is happy here. She's taken care of, has friends, a good life. Things you can't give her, not unless you clean yourself up."

"God, why does everyone think they can tell me how to live my life?"

"Because you're ruining it, and if you aren't careful, the road you're on will dead-end." She stared hard into Kendra's glassy eyes, hoping somehow she could get through to the other woman before it was too late. Leah wanted that so much for Tyler and Maddie. They deserved to have their sister and mother back.

Leah realized Kendra wasn't ready to hear anything contrary to her own self-centered worldview when she started stalking toward Leah.

"Please don't let her take me," Maddie said from where she held tight to the back of Leah's leg.

"I won't, sweetie."

"You can't keep my daughter from me."

Leah heard sirens in the distance. "I'm pretty sure the sheriff will see that differently."

Kendra jerked her head toward the sound of the sirens then back toward Leah. "You called the cops?"

She didn't wait for an answer, instead running for her car. Her boyfriend barely had time to dive into the passenger side before Kendra peeled out, spitting gravel so that it hit both Tyler's truck and Leah's car.

Tyler came toward them, breathing hard, his face bloody. "Are you two okay?"

"Yes," Leah said, though her panic was building by the moment. She'd thought she'd gotten away from the kind of violence that had sent her fleeing Houston. Though she knew it was unreasonable, seeing Tyler's power unleashed made her want to get in her car and flee yet again.

As Tyler came closer, she held up her hand to stop him. Not wanting to admit her own fear of him getting too close, she instead nodded toward where Maddie had her face pressed into Leah's side crying, then indicated the blood on Tyler's face.

He looked at her for a moment, and she wondered if she hadn't hidden her own fear as well as she'd tried to. But then he nodded.

"Take Maddie into the house. I'll take care of things out here," he said, indicating the two sheriff's department vehicles now racing toward them up the driveway.

"Come on, sweetie." Leah bent and picked up Maddie, who clung to Leah as if afraid her mother would come back and steal her away.

Leah understood that feeling of needing to cling

to something safe, something that would protect her. So she didn't release Maddie when she got inside, instead heading straight for the couch and continuing to hold Maddie close.

"Shh, it's okay. You're safe now."

"I thought she would take me and make me go back. I'd never see you and Uncle Tyler again. Or Baxter and Felix."

At the sound of their names, the pups parked themselves at the edge of the couch. Baxter propped his front paws on the edge of the couch cushion and whined.

"I think someone wants to see if you're okay."

Maddie turned to look but didn't immediately release Leah's neck.

"I'm right here," she said, reassuring Maddie that simply letting go of her wouldn't make her and her ability to protect Maddie disappear.

Maddie reached over and lifted Baxter onto her lap. Seeing poor little Felix down on the floor, unable to pull himself up yet, Leah mirrored Maddie's action and lifted Felix onto her own lap. They were all still there, taking comfort from each other, when Conner and Tyler came inside a few minutes later. She could hear Sheriff Simon Teague outside talking into his radio. Though she couldn't make out the words, she suspected it had to do with Kendra and her brute of a boyfriend.

"I see you all are in good hands," Conner said with a smile. "Or should I say paws?"

Maddie shrank closer to Leah's side.

"It's okay, sweetie," Leah said. "This is my cousin, Conner. He's a deputy sheriff."

"Is that like a policeman?"

Conner smiled as he crouched on the other side of the coffee table. "Exactly. You're a smart girl. So smart that I wondered if you knew the answer to a couple of questions I have."

Conner asked if Maddie knew her mom's boy-friend's name or the names of any of her mom's other friends. Maddie shared what little she knew.

"Very good." Conner pulled out his ticket book and wrote something in it. Then he ripped it out and gave it to Maddie. "The next time you're in town, have your uncle or Leah bring you by the sheriff's department. I'll give you a tour and then I'll treat you to an ice-cream cone. How does that sound?"

"Good." Maddie's voice sounded so small that Leah worried she might go silent again.

Leah caught the slight motion of Conner's head toward Tyler, who'd washed his face clean of blood before coming inside, though it was still obvious he'd been in a fight.

Tyler walked toward the couch and sank to one knee in front of Maddie. "Come on, sweetie. Let's go upstairs so Leah can talk to Conner, okay?"

"Is Mommy going to come back to take me?"

Tyler's big hand swallowed Maddie's knee when he placed it there. "I won't let anyone take you. I promise you that."

Leah hoped that was a promise he could keep. Surely after what had happened, no court would send Maddie back to her mother. But would they take her away from her uncle? Not if there was any justice in the world.

Maddie looked up at Leah then back at Tyler. "Can Leah spend the night with us tonight?"

"I think that's a good idea," Tyler said, surprising Leah. He'd been so careful not to do anything that might hint at impropriety while he sought to get custody of Maddie.

"I—"

"That is a good idea," Conner said. "I suspect they're long gone, but just to be on the safe side."

Leah met her cousin's gaze and she saw his concern. He was probably wondering how the events of the day were affecting her considering her previous brush with violence.

"I'll be okay," she said, but even she heard the waver in her voice.

"I'd feel better if we were all under one roof tonight," Tyler said.

"Either that or I'm taking you to Mom and Dad's," Conner added.

Though she felt they were ganging up on her, she had to admit the idea of going back to the bunkhouse tonight made her want to vomit.

Maddie placed her little hand on Leah's thigh. "Please stay here. Baxter and Felix want you to stay, too."

Leah smiled and scratched both pups between the ears. "Well, how can I say no to that?"

Conner waited until Tyler had taken Maddie up to her room before he sank onto the coffee table in front of Leah.

"Are you okay?"

She nodded. "Shaken, but I was more concerned about Maddie."

"And Tyler?"

"Of course. He's the only steady person in Maddie's life."

"That's not what I mean, and I think you know that."

She ran her fingers back through her hair. "Is that why you said I should stay here tonight? You playing matchmaker, too?"

"No, my first concern is your safety, and I trust Tyler to provide that. But if there's something else going on, I'm okay with that, too."

Leah felt weird talking to Conner about her love life, so she changed the topic. "Do you really think Kendra and her boyfriend won't come back?"

"If she has a lick of sense she won't."

"I'm not going to place money on that."

"Tyler will have this place locked up tight tonight, and I'm going to make sure we have regular patrols out this way all night. We've already got an APB out on them."

"Did they legally do anything wrong? I mean Kendra is Maddie's mother and has custody."

"We can charge them with child endangerment. Tyler told me he's trying to get custody of Maddie. Simon and I will do whatever we can to make sure that happens."

"Thank you."

After Conner had her recount the events from her point of view, he stood and headed for the door. She followed him so that she could lock it behind him. Conner paused halfway out the door and met her gaze. He nodded toward the stairs.

"Tyler is a good man, willing to protect those he loves. You deserve that. You deserve to be happy."

As she listened to Conner drive away, his words echoed in her head. Just that morning, she would have gladly agreed. But in the wake of the violence in Tyler's front yard, with him taking part, she had to wonder if the idea of a calm, peaceful life with a man she loved was nothing more than an unobtainable dream.

Chapter Fifteen

Tyler looked across the table at Leah. How quiet she'd been since Conner left reminded him of when Maddie had arrived at his house. When he'd come back downstairs, leaving Maddie to color in her room, she'd been in the kitchen fixing a quick dinner of grilled ham and cheese sandwiches and tomato soup. He thought of the menu as more suitable to a winter day, but he didn't say so. She'd seemed to need something to do, so he let her.

When he'd asked if she was okay, she'd nodded and quickly answered, "I'm fine." It hadn't been very believable. He'd been left standing there wondering what the right move was—press her to talk or let her process what had happened at her own pace, deciding on her own when or if she wanted to talk about it.

It didn't help that Maddie was back to her quiet ways tonight, too. He silently cursed Kendra yet again. Why had she shown up to drag her unwilling child away from a place where she was happy? Did his sister hate him that much? If so, why leave Maddie with him in the first place? He dropped half of his sandwich back onto his plate, losing what little appetite he'd had. He had to stop asking questions to which he wasn't going to find any satisfactory answers.

Needing to do something besides sit in the deathly quiet kitchen fuming that his sister had dropped yet another bomb into the middle of his life, he scooted back his chair and directed his attention to Maddie, who was obviously done eating and had moved on to picking apart her napkin and depositing the bits of paper in her soup bowl.

"Come on, kiddo. Time for bed."

"I'll take her."

The speed and urgency with which Leah stood threw a punch right to the middle of Tyler's heart. She'd been a witness to more violence today, some of which he'd doled out, and now she was scared of him again. She'd seen him fight another man almost his size and walk away with no more than a few cuts and bruises, so she had to be calculating the amount of damage he could do to her when she was a fraction of his size. And the thought made him sick.

As Leah accompanied Maddie upstairs, he cleaned up the kitchen, barely containing the need to vent his anger by breaking every dish in the room. He cared about Leah. Damn it, he might even love her. If Kendra had ruined what might have been his only chance with Leah, he'd never forgive his sister. Kendra might destroy her own life, but he was sick and tired of her collateral damage.

After he disposed of the uneaten food and washed the dishes, he prowled the lower level of the house like a zoo animal relegated to an enclosure a miniscule percentage of the size of its normal range. He needed space, to burn off his anger, but he wasn't willing to leave Leah and Maddie in the house alone. His gut told him his sister wouldn't come back again so soon, but he still wasn't taking any chances.

Plus, he needed to talk to Leah, to find out what she was thinking before it drove him insane wondering.

But Leah didn't come downstairs. When after nearly an hour had passed without a sign of her, he eased up the steps and peeked around the doorway leading into Maddie's room.

The small bedside lamp revealed Maddie curled up facing Leah, both of them asleep. He wanted to think that Leah had agreed to stay until Maddie fell asleep and the events of the day had caused her to pass out, too. But as he looked at the two people who meant the most to him in the world, he worried that Leah had chosen to sleep on a sliver of a twin bed rather than come downstairs and face a man she now feared.

LEAH JERKED AWAKE in the middle of the night, her heart thundering with surging fear. Somehow she managed to catch herself before she cried out or moved too suddenly. Beside her, Maddie rested peacefully, Baxter nestled beside her. Leah hadn't had the heart to refuse her when Maddie had asked if Baxter could sleep in her bed instead of his, just for tonight.

Leah watched the gentle rise and fall of Maddie's breaths, envying her ability to sleep evidently free of nightmares. Leah wasn't so lucky. The scene from earlier had replayed in her dream, but this time she'd been on the receiving end of Tyler's fists instead of Mark. She knew it was irrational to think he'd ever do anything like that, but she was just going to need some time to get past this fresh wave of fear. He'd been patient with her before, and she hoped he could be again.

As the minutes and hours ticked by, she couldn't go back to sleep. Every little creak of the house, every normal night noise outside magnified in her mind to sound ominous. She was glad she'd fallen asleep with the light on because if she'd awakened in a darkened house, she might have frightened herself into a major panic attack.

Though she was unable to sleep, she didn't move, not wanting to chance waking Maddie. So she spent several hours with her mind and heart racing and her back aching from the need to stretch.

Finally, as the first hints of daylight began to paint the darkness at the window a lighter shade, she eased out of the bed. One of Baxter's eyes opened lazily about halfway. She froze until the eye shut again. Despite her inner turmoil, the little guy made her smile.

But as she descended the stairs to find Tyler asleep sitting on the couch, Felix curled up next to him, her smile faded. Not because it wasn't a sweet scene, it was, but because she wanted to go snuggle next to Tyler's other side and found herself shaking at the thought. She wanted to scream at Kendra until the other woman's ears bled for doing this to her, tainting something that was so beautiful and that had filled her heart with joy. Maybe she'd get to that point again, but she needed some time to process, to figure out if what she'd felt before Kendra's appearance was real or what she was feeling now, the familiar keyed-up anxiety, was the reality and she'd simply been living a fantasy with Tyler.

She moved toward the door, but Tyler jerked awake with such a sudden motion that she yelped before covering her mouth, hoping she hadn't woken and frightened Maddie.

"Leah, is something wrong?" Tyler was on his feet in an instant.

She took a few steps backward before she could think how that would look to him. She wasn't even sure if she would have been able to prevent it even if she'd had time to think it through.

"I'm just going home. I've got a lot of work to do today."

He didn't look as though he believed her, and she didn't blame him. She was a terrible liar. But was that any worse than telling him the truth, that at the moment she was too scared to be alone with him?

Maybe she was going insane, because that's what her rationale felt like—insanity.

"I can walk you back." Probably without realizing it, he negated his offer by glancing toward the stairs.

"No, don't leave Maddie."

When he looked back at her, she saw a mixture of sadness, longing and…loss? He had lost his only sibling. Kendra might not be dead, but what Leah had witnessed broke her heart for Tyler. Part of her wanted to walk into his arms, to give and receive comfort. But it wouldn't do either of them any good if being that close to him freaked her out like it had the night they'd first kissed. She needed to be sure that wouldn't happen, give herself time for the new fear to dissipate if it was going to.

"I'm sorry about yesterday," he said.

"It wasn't your fault."

"I'm still sorry you had to witness all the violence."

He was trying so hard, and she hated that she couldn't simply wave off what had happened and move forward from where they'd been prior to Kendra's reappearance. After all, what had she expected him to do when being attacked? Take it and let Kendra haul off a distraught Maddie like she was nothing more than an old gym bag?

Maybe when the full light of a new day washed over the ranch, all her irrational fears and the dregs of her nightmare would fade away and she could come apologize for holding him at a distance when he'd done nothing wrong. She certainly hoped that's what would happen.

But as she walked back to the bunkhouse knowing that Tyler was out on his front porch watching her, she wondered if she should get out before she got in any deeper with Tyler. Yes, she loved him, but she hadn't said it. Neither had he. Maybe he didn't even feel it. He cared, yes, but that wasn't the same as being in love with a person enough to want to spend the rest of your life with that individual.

As she shut herself inside the bunkhouse, she closed her eyes and wondered if it would be better for everyone involved if she left and started over yet again somewhere else, maybe where no one knew her and she wouldn't allow herself to be lured into trusting she was past that one night that had shattered her life. Where she wouldn't fall in love with a man who deserved someone strong enough to be with him.

TYLER DIDN'T THINK he'd ever had such a difficult time concentrating on work. He'd hesitantly taken Maddie to school that morning, but not before informing the officials at the school to be on the lookout for Kendra and Mark. When he'd stopped by the sheriff's office, there were no updates on Kendra's whereabouts. While out shoeing a horse for a customer, he'd been so distracted he'd managed to smash his finger.

Going home didn't make things any better. He hadn't seen or talked to Leah since she'd left the house early that morning. And he hadn't been able to stop torturing himself wondering what she was thinking, if she was going to leave. The longer he went without seeing her, the more convinced he became that she was going to race out of his life as quickly as she'd come into it. As quickly as she'd grown to mean a great deal to him, and to Maddie.

Not wanting to leave the main part of the ranch any more than he had to, he filled his afternoon with tasks in the barn. Cleaning stalls, replacing a broken slat on a stall, rearranging the tack room even though it didn't need it. And resisting the urge to walk up to the bunkhouse to see how Leah was doing, to make sure she was okay. But the last thing he wanted was to do something that was the last straw that would push her away. Maddie would be brokenhearted. Hell, he wouldn't fare any better.

He sank onto a bale of hay as he realized he didn't just like Leah a lot. He'd fallen in love with her. Somehow she'd walked right into an empty hole in his life that he hadn't realized was there. It was as if his life had been a puzzle with one missing piece, and she fit it perfectly. The thought of her leaving tore him up inside. He'd never felt as happy, as whole as he did when he was with her. But could he even put those feelings into words without freaking her out? Would she think it too soon to feel such things? Probably. Even he was freaked at the depth of his feelings, having never felt anything like it before.

He ended up sitting in that spot, his thoughts swirling, until it was time to go pick up Maddie. And today of all days, he didn't want to be late.

He just hoped that when they got back home, Leah was still there.

THE BUZZING OF Leah's phone on her coffee table woke her from a dead sleep. She jerked upright on the couch, her mind fuzzy. She'd fallen asleep? On the couch? How long had she been asleep?

Felix's head popped up from where he was lying in his bed. It filtered into her brain that if Felix was so content, there likely wasn't any immediate danger.

She grabbed her phone and saw it was Reina calling.

"Hey," she answered.

"Um, hey. What's wrong?"

Leah smoothed her hair back, wondering if she had a crazy head of bed hair. "Nothing. Why?"

"I don't know. You sounded startled or out of breath or something."

"I was asleep."

"In the afternoon? You're not a napper unless you're sick."

"I didn't sleep well last night. I guess it caught up to me."

"Okay, out with it. And don't even pretend there's nothing wrong because I know you better than that."

Reina was right. She did know Leah well. Plus, there was the whole thing Leah had with not being able to lie worth a darn.

Needing to share with someone, she launched into everything that had happened since they'd last spoken. Her relationship with Tyler, how much she adored Maddie, how Tyler had said she should take part in the arts and crafts trail, everything up to and including Kendra's attempt to take Maddie and Leah's resurgence of irrational fear when she'd seen Tyler punching Kendra's boyfriend. After she was finished, Reina didn't immediately answer. Leah wondered if she'd nodded off or if she'd talked so long that Reina had reached her due date and was off giving birth.

"You still there?"

"Yeah."

"Okay," Leah said, drawing out the word.

"I'm just trying to figure out how to say this without sounding mean."

"That doesn't sound good."

"I know you've been through a lot, and I've supported whatever you needed to do to heal, even move away from your best friend when she looks like a blimp."

"You're gorgeous and you know it."

"Yeah, whatever. You know I love you, but you're being ridiculous."

"Ouch."

"You need to hear this because I want you to be happy. And from what you just told me, Tyler makes you happy. Honestly, he sounds like the best thing since chocolate cake. Damn, now I want chocolate cake. Anyway, you said it yourself, the fear of him and what he could do to you is irrational. He's shown you no indication at all that he would ever hurt you. From what you just told me, it sounds like he might just very well love you as much as you love him."

"He hasn't said that."

"Neither have you. Yes, you've been hurt and are understandably wary, but so has he. He's basically lost his entire family, except for Maddie. Imagine if your parents were gone, Conner, your aunt and uncle. Would you be quick to put your heart on the line?"

Leah let the words sink in. "Why do you have to be so smart in addition to gorgeous? It's really annoying."

Reina laughed on the other end of the line.

"I know all this stuff rationally, but how do I deal with fear when it's irrational?"

"Give it the middle finger. In fact, give it two and tell it to get the hell out of your life. You're done with it."

"That may be easier said than done."

"You won't know until you try. Plus I sort of like the image of you flipping double birds and going after what you want. I may not be able to see you right now, but I can tell you that just listening to you talk about Tyler...he's what you want. And you need to tell him that and, as they say, let the chips fall where they may."

Tears of gratitude pooled in Leah's eyes. "Thank you. You're the best friend ever."

"Remember you said that when I have squalling infants and need a mommy break."

"On-call babysitting, you've got it."

After Leah hung up, she went to the kitchen and nabbed a chocolate chip cookie she'd made earlier when she hadn't been able to concentrate on work or even sit still. Munching on the cookie, she paced the bunkhouse, noting the personal touches she'd added in her time there. It really did feel like home, and she didn't want to leave.

She wasn't going to.

A wave of unexpected self-empowerment rushed over her as she made that decision. She was tired of being afraid, and she was going to marshal all her willpower to defeat the fear. It would not win. Jason Garton would not win.

Leah was going to win.

That decision made, she paced some more as she ran through different ways to tell Tyler everything she wanted to say. Needed to say. By the time night cloaked the world outside, she figured she just had to march herself down to the house and go with whatever came out of her mouth. Otherwise, she was going to drive herself bonkers, not to mention wear crisscrossing trenches in the bunkhouse floor.

She took the time to shower and change into fresh clothes, then inhaled a deep breath before stepping out onto the porch. She waited for the panic brought

A Rancher to Love

about by the darkness to slam into her, but it didn't. Yes, there was a buzz of anxiety, but she wasn't in full-blown panic. Pushing forward, she stepped off the porch and headed down the driveway.

I will not be afraid. There's nothing here to hurt me. No one is lurking in the dark on the off chance I'd walk down the driveway in the dark.

When she reached the yard in front of Tyler's house, she nearly cried in relief. Anyone who didn't know what she'd been through would have no idea how big of an accomplishment her short walk had been. She took a moment to soak it in, looking back up the driveway and laughing under her breath at the memory of what Reina had said about flipping the fear a double bird. Leah found she didn't have to.

She took a deep breath and let it out slowly, more nervous about talking to Tyler than the walk through the dark. She stepped up onto the porch and knocked on the door. Despite Baxter's bark, it took Tyler several moments to appear. When he finally opened the door, he seemed relieved. She hadn't even thought that he might wonder if it was Kendra or Mark at the door. But they didn't really seem like the type to politely knock.

"Did Conner call you, too?"

"What?"

Evidently seeing that she didn't know what he was talking about, he opened the door wider and invited her in. Maddie bounded in from the kitchen, and Leah suddenly wished she'd brought the cookies she'd made.

"I missed you," Maddie said and ran over to hug Leah. Her eyes misting, Leah hugged the girl back. "I missed you, too." Strangely, though she'd seen Maddie only last night, she had missed her. Leah sure hoped her conversation with Tyler went well.

But when she turned to see him tense and his mind far away, she worried that maybe she'd reacted badly one too many times. Deciding not to give up before she'd even really tried, she crouched in front of Maddie. "Do you mind playing while your uncle and I go talk for a few minutes?"

"Okay." Just like that, Maddie turned her attention to Baxter and started coaxing him up the stairs.

"Let's go outside," Tyler said and headed for the door without looking at her.

Was he really that upset with her? He hadn't seemed upset that morning when she'd left the house, but maybe he'd had time to stew all day and felt differently now. Only one way to find out.

Once they were outside, Tyler proceeded away from the house toward where his truck was parked. Once there, he braced his hands against the side of the bed.

"I just got off the phone with Conner. Kendra and Mark were arrested about an hour ago near Fort Worth. They're being charged with DUI, resisting arrest and possession of drug paraphernalia. There will be more charges locally."

She moved toward him and placed her hand against his back. "I'm so sorry, Tyler."

He shook his head. "No, it's a good thing. If she's locked up, she'll be forced to get clean and away from her creep boyfriend." He took a deep breath. "And Maddie will be safe."

Tyler pushed away from the truck and faced her, crossing his arms.

"I totally understand if you don't want to be a part of this mess. If you want to move, I won't charge you any rent. And I can help you, or if you'd prefer I can find someone else."

She couldn't listen to this anymore. She stepped forward and placed her palms against the bulk of his crossed arms. "I didn't come down here to tell you I was moving."

"You didn't?"

"I'll admit this morning I did think about it. But with the help of a good friend, I realized that's not what I want."

"It's not?" He sounded like he wasn't sure whether to believe her.

"No, it's not. I've thought about nothing else all day. What I want more than anything in the world is you, Tyler." Now for the big reveal. "I've fallen in love with you. You and Maddie and this ranch, my new life. It's everything I never knew I wanted. And every bit of it has made me believe that I can move beyond what happened to me and have a good life, a happy life. But I understand it's fast and that you might not feel—"

"I love you, too."

Leah froze, not sure she'd heard him correctly. But when he pulled her into his arms and kissed her, she thought maybe she had.

When they finally stopped to breathe, Tyler pulled back enough to look at her. "You're really not leaving?"

"Not unless you want me to."

"That's the last thing I want." He ran his thumb across her cheek and looked at her with an expression that really did make her feel loved. "We'll go as slowly as you want, but I'm going to be honest with you. I feel like you're already part of this family, and I want to make that real at some point."

She swallowed. "Are you saying what I think you are?"

"If you think that someday I want to make you my wife, then yes. But there's no hurry. I want you to be ready, and I want to do things right."

Leah had the crazy idea that she was ready now, but she thought it was probably a good plan to take their time. With Maddie safe and neither of them going anywhere, they hopefully had all the time in the world.

"Thank you," she said.

"For?"

"For everything. Picnics by the creek, horseback rides, fixing hot water heaters, making me laugh, understanding when I was having a hard time conquering my fear." She ran her hands slowly up his arms. "And you're pretty good in bed, too, if I remember correctly."

"That right? Maybe I need to refresh your memory."

"Sounds like a good idea." She grew more serious. "Thank you for helping me get my life back."

He kissed her softly. "Thank you for filling the spot in mine I didn't know was empty."

As they kissed beneath a gorgeous late summer sky, Leah's heart overflowed with love until it filled the rest of her body and outward to envelop the night around her. It wasn't scary anymore because she was safe and in control of her life. And even more important was the fact that with Tyler, her heart was safe, as well.

* * * * *

Look for THE COWBOY TAKES A WIFE,
the next book in Trish Milburn's
BLUE FALLS, TEXAS *series in October 2016!*
Available wherever Harlequin books
and ebooks are sold.

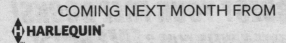
#1605 A BULL RIDER'S PRIDE
Welcome to Ramblewood • by Amanda Renee
After a stay in the hospital, bull rider Brady Sawyer can't get back into the arena fast enough. Which is against the advice of Sheila Lindstrom, the doctor who put Brady back together...and could possibly break his heart!

#1606 TEXAS REBELS: PHOENIX
Texas Rebels • by Linda Warren
Everything is changing for Phoenix Rebel. Not only has the formerly carefree cowboy discovered he's the father to a baby boy, he's also fallen in love with Rosemary McCray—a sworn enemy of his family.

#1607 COURTED BY THE COWBOY
The Boones of Texas • by Sasha Summers
Kylee James keeps people at arm's length for good reasons. Especially Fisher Boone. With her past dogging her, Kylee knows the handsome cowboy deserves happiness, which is something she could never give him...

#1608 THE KENTUCKY COWBOY'S BABY
Angel Crossing, Arizona • by Heidi Hormel
Former bull rider AJ McCreary has inherited a ranch in Arizona and the timing is perfect—he needs to get off the rodeo circuit to properly raise his toddler daughter. Problem is, Pepper Bourne thinks his ranch belongs to her!

SPECIAL EXCERPT FROM

H HARLEQUIN®
™

Western Romance

Brady Sawyer almost died the last time he rode a bull, and now he's determined to compete again. Can surgeon Sheila Lindstrom risk her heart on a man who cares so little for the life she saved?

Read on for a sneak preview of
A BULL RIDER'S PRIDE,
the latest book in Amanda Renee's popular
WELCOME TO RAMBLEWOOD *series.*

"This can't happen again." Sheila squared her shoulders. "It happened, we got it out of our systems, we don't mention it to each other or anyone else. I could lose my job over that kiss."

"Then, you're fired."

"I'm what?" Sheila laughed. "You can't fire me as your physician, Brady."

"Actually, I can. You're telling me us being together is an issue because you're my doctor. I'm eliminating the problem."

"It's not that simple," Sheila said. "Grace General Hospital frowns on doctors dating former patients. I'd lose the respect of my colleagues. And if you run to my attending and have me removed as your doctor, it will raise a few red flags. I put my entire life on hold to become a doctor. I'm not throwing it away for a fling. Dedication and devotion from people like me are the reason you're alive today."

"Sheila, I respect your career. I admire your dedication and achievements." If she only understood that he'd devoted the same energy to his own career.

She scoffed. "You take everything for granted. I helped give you a second chance at life. A second chance to see your son grow up, and you want to throw it all away for pride."

"It's not pride. I have to earn a living to support my son." Brady sat down beside her. "Gunner is everything to me."

"Gunner doesn't care what you do for a living. He's four! He loves you no matter what." Sheila threw her hands in the air. "Okay, I'm done with this conversation. I don't care what you do." She stood and reached for the doorknob, then hesitated. She slammed her fist into her thigh. "So help me, I do care." She spun to face him. "That's the problem. I care what happens to you."

Brady hadn't expected Sheila to admit her feelings for him. He'd suspected and even hoped the attraction was mutual. But hearing the words, the connection between them took on a completely different meaning. How could he walk away from a woman who intrigued him like no other?

He reached for her hand. "This is all I know how to be—a bull rider. A rodeo cowboy."

"You're so much more than that," Sheila whispered.

Don't miss
A BULL RIDER'S PRIDE
by Amanda Renee, available August 2016 wherever
Harlequin® Western Romance
books and ebooks are sold.

www.Harlequin.com

Wrangle Your Friends for the
Ultimate Ranch Girls' Getaway

**Win an all-expenses-paid 3-night luxurious
stay for you and your 3 guests at
The Resort at Paws Up in Greenough, Montana.**

Retail Value $10,000

A TOAST TO FRIENDSHIP,
AN ADVENTURE OF A LIFETIME!

Learn more at
www.Harlequinranchgetaway.com

Sweepstakes ends August 31, 2016

HARLEQUIN®

A *Romance* FOR EVERY MOOD™

JUST CAN'T GET ENOUGH?

Join our social communities
and talk to us online.

You will have access to the latest
news on upcoming titles and special
promotions, but most importantly,
you can talk to other fans about your
favorite Harlequin reads.

Harlequin.com/Community

 Facebook.com/HarlequinBooks

Twitter.com/HarlequinBooks

Pinterest.com/HarlequinBooks

HARLEQUIN®

A *Romance* FOR EVERY MOOD™

**Stay up-to-date on all your
romance-reading news with the
Harlequin Shopping Guide,
featuring bestselling authors, exciting new
miniseries, books to watch and more!**

The newest issue will be delivered right to you
with our compliments! There are 4 each year.

Signing up is easy.

EMAIL

ShoppingGuide@Harlequin.ca

WRITE TO US

HARLEQUIN BOOKS
Attention: Customer Service Department
P.O. Box 9057, Buffalo, NY 14269-9057

OR PHONE

1-800-873-8635 in the United States
1-888-343-9777 in Canada

Please allow 4-6 weeks for delivery of the first issue by mail.